Esther Bernon Carpenter

South-county Neighbors

Esther Bernon Carpenter

South-county Neighbors

ISBN/EAN: 9783337001285

Printed in Europe, USA, Canada, Australia, Japan

Cover: Foto ©Andreas Hilbeck / pixelio.de

More available books at **www.hansebooks.com**

SOUTH-COUNTY NEIGHBORS

BY

ESTHER BERNON CARPENTER

———◆———

BOSTON
ROBERTS BROTHERS
1887

TO

OLIVER WENDELL HOLMES,

MY EARLIEST AND LATEST MASTER,

I Dedicate

THIS BOOK.

PREFACE.

THE busy life of the South County of to-day still keeps certain wholesomely rustic phases of its leisurely yesterday. But in choosing the subjects of my character-studies I have generally preferred to set back the hands of the town-clocks until they pointed to the time of forty or fifty years ago, when everybody's hobby was ridden bare-backed, and when freaks and oddities of individuality flourished unchecked by an upstart civilization.

In those generous days the bucolic and seafaring types ran to a luxuriant growth. The informal club of rural fellowship met at the country store, where the talk flowed in a vein of wiseacre moralizing, or of delicious inconsequence, and the season of expansion was equally improved by the talkers, the listeners, and by those no less sincere seekers after social influences who yet remained among the inarticulate intelligences, and dwelt in a contemplation

which seemed to yield the fruits of a Yankee
Nirvâna.

Loitering on the highway, or sharing the
charitable hospitality of the farmhouse, came
and went "all the vagrant train" that were
known to the hamlet of Lissoy. The classi-
cally familiar figures of "the aged beggar,"
"the broken soldier," or "the ruined spend-
thrift," appeared by their New England representatives, — such as infirm-witted "old travellers," waifs from the War of 1812, and blighted
scions of good families.

All roads ranged by these picturesque origi-
nals led to the "town-farm," where they were as
rudely assorted and classified as any set of
grotesquely-carved and half-broken toys that
are hastily crowded into a box. Here were
types of no distant kindred to those of the rural
almshouse of Crabbe, or the gathering of "ran-
die, gangrel bodies" at Poosie Nancy's; and all
were thoughtfully grouped by the village fathers
into a kind of Conservatory of Outlawry.

Such were some of the primitive elements
entering into the life of those country "Neighbors" whose traits I have slightly indicated.

I have so entitled my book not only from the
universal neighborliness of country people, but
because this title of "neighbor" has been commonly used among us with a scope of expression which makes it the equivalent of the

Western " stranger," as a genial and conciliatory form of address, suiting either the oldest acquaintance or the latest comer.

Those who best know our Narragansett country, and have already become familiar with these " South-County Folks " as they made their occasional appearances in the " Providence Journal " will least need the assurance that the figures of my studies are simply types, rather than likenesses. To others — to those present strangers in whom every writer anxiously hopes to find future friends, — I can only commend my people for the sake of that reality in the power of which they lived and moved in my consciousness, so that I looked into their faces, heard their voices, and knew no rest from these persistent guests until I had suffered them to tell their stories.

Wakefield, Washington County,
Rhode Island, *May* 10, 1887.

CONTENTS.

SOUTH-COUNTY NEIGHBORS.

———◆———

SALLY OF THE SOUTH COUNTY.

NO maiden of ballad romance was she, but
simply our ancient Yankee maid-of-all-
work, — a " help " of the old-fashioned, pains-
taking sort, who gave herself to the household
routine with an unflagging zeal and energy.
She was a natural ascetic (if that is not a con-
tradiction in terms), a rigid economist, and
though the kitchen over which she presided as
tutelary deity was always filled with the smoke
and steam of sacrifice, she conscientiously con-
sumed her failures in cookery, — invariably
making choice, for her own meals, of the burnt
johnny-cake and the "slack-baked" bread.
When remonstrated with, she generally indulged
in the terse reply that "wicked waste makes
woeful want."

One of my most characteristic recollections of
Sally dimly shows her wrapped in the incense
arising from a frying-pan of doughnuts, while
she served as a grim target for the pleasantries

of the village doctor, who never omitted her in his visits to the house, always having the same time-worn jest to proffer anent some very recent widower, or some particularly aged and forlorn bachelor swain, to whom he was about to recommend her as a housekeeper. To what phase of even a middle-aged vanity these railleries could possibly minister is now, as then, a mystery; but if the doctor's jokes could hardly be counted as instances of delicate homage, graceful attention, or well-turned compliment, I suppose that at least they stood as the equivalents of those unknown quantities in the life of Sally.

As to my knowledge of Sally, however, I cannot boast of any nearer acquaintance with her than that of being received on what I may call the frigid and precarious terms of a tolerated intimacy. I was naturally much attached to her society and her doughnuts, and though, in her own vigorous language, she "would n't have children always 'round underfoot," she consoled me with dazzling promises which soothed my simple credulity with anticipations of a visit we should make to a metropolis known to me, by ear, under the phonetic formula of "Branzinewuks," but which I have since found to be absurdly written Brand's Iron Works. This youthful vision was never realized, and I fear that I must some day make my own the lament of the aged peasant

who was never able to accomplish the cherished
wish of his life, in visiting the capital of his native
province.

> " Oh ! fate is spun and life is run,
> And I have not seen Carcassonne ; "

for, as the poet of this lyric muses, —

> " Each mortal has his Carcassonne."

But I sometimes went with Sally to attend the
funerals of the neighbors. Seen from our post
of observation, as humble and unrelated sym-
pathizers, they were occasions of solemn agitation and subdued bustle. The collection of
" teams " in the door-yard, the horses being
taken out of the shafts and tied, suggested the
same signs of a gathering crowd at an auction.
Women and children filled the rooms ; the men
were chiefly grouped in the entries, looking in
at the windows, or standing by the door. The
outward tokens of woe in dress or otherwise
were few or none. There was no music, and
there were no flowers, except in the small nose-
gays carried by some of the nervous women, as
rustic substitutes for the vinaigrette of fashion,
and made up of " lemon balm," with " boys' love"
and lavender, or perhaps a sprig of sweet basil,
according to choice. The smell of varnish from
the newly-made, freshly-stained pine coffin was
penetrating. So was the voice of the exhorter,
as from his station behind the light-stand, on

which was placed a large Bible, he, for an hour
or more, continued to " improve the occasion,"
and if successful, was approved as having said
everything he could to " harrow up the feelings " of any persons who might be supposed
insensible to the teachings of death; the whole
closing with a prayer, in which every relative of
the deceased, present or absent, must be remem-
bered, or lasting offence would be given. Then
the undertaker rose to say that an opportunity
would now be offered for the relations and
friends of the corpse to take a last parting look.
This was a long ceremony, beginning with the
leave-taking of the family; but at last all the
distant acquaintances, the slow-moving old folk,
and the young mothers, with little children in
their arms, had made their deliberate way
through the room, and the neighbors who acted
as bearers removed the coffin, first with a matter-
of-fact coolness placing their hats upon it, after
the lid had been audibly screwed down by the
undertaker in the stern and uncompromising
old way. These good, severe people tasted
griefs more thoroughly than joys, and would
have held it unrighteous to abate one jot or one
tittle of the salutary dread to be inspired by the
scene. One of the early departures from this
general law, the innovation of replacing the
shroud by the ordinary dress, was at first regarded as an impiety. It obviously impaired

the force of allusion in such a remonstrance as
that addressed by the aged Quaker preacher to
the young girl who was learning a worldly art
of needlework: "Dorothy, thee won't need any
lace to be laid out in;" to which she fear-
lessly replied, with a touch of that spiritual
wisdom which belongs to babes: "No, Aunt
Huldy; but I sha'n't need any Quaker bonnet,
either." And now the neighbor who, with much
busy self-importance, "managed the funeral,"
under a request from the family which carried
all the honor of a high compliment, standing in
the doorway, read the names of the related
families, according to a jealously-arranged order
of precedence. The remains were conveyed in
a farm-wagon; the procession walked the short
distance to the spot of interment on the land of
the deceased, uninclosed it might be, and
almost certainly containing graves as yet unmarked by stones. Very young children often
failed to receive such memorials. No services
were held at the grave, as such an observance
would have savored too strongly of the superstition of priestly rites; and few heads were
uncovered; but the elder discharged the duty
of publicly inviting the bearers to dinner; and
other friends were less formally bidden to the
funeral feast. So, with a strange mingling of
the gloomy and the abhorrent, of the tasteless
and the grotesque, of the sympathetic and the

matter-of-fact in the customs of the scene, we buried our old neighbor.

Sally was not a regular attendant at any meeting, and if she had ever paid homage to any personal ideals, they were not found among the elders, whom she was accustomed to satirize, — especially one of these sons of thunder, as his flock had once delighted to call him, but of whom she gave a very trenchant account on her return from his preaching. He brought the habits of his week-day labors into the sanctuary, and the better to excel in his fervid style of oratory, took off his coat and mounted the pulpit in the costume of the hayfield. A division had appeared in his church, and his popularity was waning. Breathing out threatenings and slaughter, like Saul, against the disturbers of his peace, he finally abandoned the ground of Scriptural warning, falling into the anti-climax of quoting the language of revolutionary minstrelsy. The well-to-do farmers of his church who were in opposition to him were indicated under these poetic figures: —

> " There is a wealthy people,
>   Who sojourn in that land;
>   Their churches, all with steeples,
>   Most delicately stand.
>   Their houses, like the gilly,
>   Are painted red and gay;
>   They flourish like the lily,
>   In North America."

And in pointed attack upon the church council which was soon to sit, and from which he
expected hostilities, he closed with a vigorous
application of the colonial menace: —

> "Ye Parliament of England,
>   And Lords and Commons too,
> Consider well what you're about,
>   And what you mean to do!"

These apt quotations are partly drawn from
the popular verses on "American Taxation,"
written by a Connecticut schoolmaster, and long
since enrolled among the curiosities of our
literature.

As I said, Sally was not very desirous of my
company, unless, indeed, I could be more like a
certain little sister of hers, — whom I deemed
fabulous, but who in Sally's recital loved to wipe
dishes, and to sew her "stent," and who had
pieced out a counterpane of five hundred blocks
when she died, aged seven. But on Seventh
Day (for Sally's early habits had been formed
by the Sabbatic sect), or in seasons of afternoon
leisure, I was allowed in her room, and could
attend what might be called her *levée en prin-
cesse.* At any rate, it was her time for changing
her calico gown for a delaine one. Her sharp,
decisive, angular movements were never more
appalling than in that part of her toilette which
consisted in laying violent hands· on her hair.
We know from poetry, rather better than from

2

observation, how charming a sight it is when
Inez unbinds her dark tresses, and they fall
about her in a shadowy eclipse, until the arrowy
comb divides the flow of the sable river, and the
straight white parting gleams upon it, "one
moonbeam from the forehead to the crown."
But such was not precisely the picture suggested
by the excellent Sally as she stood ruthlessly
grasping her rather harsh hair, while seizing
upon some hairpins of giant stature, and of firm
and resolute aspect, which she adjusted with the
air of a carpenter at his nail-driving, crowning
the whole with the huge square-topped horn
comb which was coeval with her youth. The
finished result gave the damsel a somewhat forbidding appearance, and was painfully suggestive of an inability to close her eyes. I do not
remember that Sally ever went through this
beautifying process without inveighing against
the modern extravagance of using hairpins. In
her early days she had been well suited with the
thorns of the locust tree, or those of the haw-
thorn; and she was also a stickler for the merits
of the garb of her girlhood, the long-unused
"petticoat and cooler," or, short sack, which
made up the nearest approach to a peasant costume that was ever worn by Yankee girls. Yet
some slight tokens of vanity Sally still retained.
She wore in her ears the thin gold hoops that
had been the work of her brother, a jeweller's

apprentice; and in her less disapproving moods
she would display to me the unsunned glories of
that impressive structure of black silk, decked
with a bunch of fiercely blushing cherries, which
for the last ten years had held the prestige of
being her best bonnet.

The library which sufficed for her mental
needs consisted of a certain fetich, carefully pre-
served under the title of the Good Book, with
the town tax-book, and by way of light literature, a pious tract describing the sufferings and
deaths of the successive Mrs. Adoniram Judsons.
Sally had a numerous acquaintance among the
Second Adventists and the Millerites, but they
had never been able to impart any touch of their
dangerous enthusiasm to her dry and self-con-
tained nature.   With matter-of-fact composure,
or with grim humor, she detailed the particulars
of their several disappointments in the time of
the dissolution of our planet, and in the fit of
their ascension-robes.   Indeed, I never heard
her commit herself to any profession of religious
faith, unless the occasional expression of a conservative confidence in the efficiency of "them
that rules all things" may be regarded as such.
Like George Eliot's Dolly Winthrop, she invariably referred to the heavenly powers by darkly
remote plural pronouns.   She sometimes had
me read the Bible to her, while she pursued her
stated Sunday occupation of ", putting to rights"

her chest of drawers. She rarely indicated any
choice of chapters. It was all good, she would
say in a tone of didactic reproof at any proposal
of selection; but I think she inclined to the intricate style of Saint Paul, and our readings were
frequently from Romans. With greater zest,
however, she scanned the tax-book, of which
she was an annual recipient, as she proudly paid
a tax of one dollar and a quarter on her maternal
homestead, a fragment of a house, as dilapidated
as any old hat thrown away by the roadside, and
out of the broken windows of which popped the
heads of negro children as you went by. Sally's
ancient father, who lived with a married daughter, had been a soldier in the War of 1812, and by
all his acquaintances was scrupulously addressed
by the brevet title of General. His military
training had certainly taught him to obey, for
he was domineered over by every inmate of the
house, down to his youngest granddaughter,
who was Sally's especial aversion. " That there
gal's as spry as a kildee," was his delighted
boast, provoking thereby a scornful sniff from
Sally, who hated all praises, and the withering
remark that she was a sight smarter to play than
what she was to work. " Come, come, Sarai,"
the indulgent old grandsire pleaded, "she ain't
but a little mite of a gal." I have heard many
more impressive remarks since, but few, I think,
that have left a pleasanter memory of the sim-

plicity of human kindness than these words of
the old man, who was in what Dr. Holmes calls
the saccharine stage of life, when the temper
overflows in sweetness at a touch, as the maple
tree yields its sugar on being tapped. I am
afraid it is not an experience of every life.

Sally was wont to refresh herself, while knitting in her own room, by singing, in a voice which
I hope had known better days, such edifying
snatches of hymnody as —

> "Oh! won't we have a happy time,
>   When we arrive at home ;
> A-eating honey and a-drinking wine,
>   When we arrive at home !"

Somehow I could not fancy Sally as anything
but an incongruous figure at a banquet; and I
knew she had a mortal antipathy to honey; but
that seemed not in the least to detract from the
zest with which she continued to make merry in
her spiritual song.

"Sally, when will they arrive at home?" I
finally propounded.

"What say, darter?"

This was an unusually affectionate form of address from Sally, but I suppose she was mol-
lified by the enlivening imagery of her sacred
ditty.

"I want to know when they will get home."

"Why they'm all coming back, to reign a
thousand years."

"Shall we be here then, Sally?"

"Land o' cakes! yes, child. We'm the wicked, 'n' the wicked has all got to be burnt up, you know; 'n' we shall be ashes under the soles of the feet of the righteous in them days — by their tell. I d'n know 's I know," pursued Sally. "Some folks talks one way, 'n' some another," she concluded dispassionately, settling her knitting-sheath for another bout, and drawing on the ball of yarn which she kept in the large old-fashioned pocket of woollen stuff which always hung at her waist, as a survival of the half-colonial dress of her early days.

I have since renewed my acquaintance with Sally's camp-meeting chorus, or with strains not unlike it, in the stories of Miss Prescott, who associated them with a Christian society of high repute for devotional fervor and missionary zeal. Similar instances of a graceful unbending on the part of the saints may be studied in that curious collection of the favorite New-Light tunes, with other psalmody of the South County, published under the title of the "Bible Harp."

I regret to say that an estrangement finally occurred between Sally and myself. The friendship which had borne the strain of pronounced theological differences could not outlast the ordeal of political bitterness. We were divided in opinion upon the merits of the Presidential candidates. Sally was naturally a supporter of a certain "old Bluecannon," as he was seriously known, not only in our nursery politics, but among his partisans of the circle at the village store. I suppose I thought him little better than Bluebeard. I could not attend the flag-raising, as it was no more suitable an occasion for the appearance of pretty-behaved little girls than the circus itself; but my cousins had faithfully drilled me in their frantic war-whoop of "Fremont and Freedom! Jessie and the Union!" and we dinned it in the ears of our elders until, as I almost think, their cherished Republican principles trembled to the foundations.

Poor dear Sally, how good you were, in your way, and what an unlovely way it was! but the last word now spoken of you shall be the frank confession that your young companion of those days would have done well if she had studied the example afforded by the rude strength of a nature that was generous in deeds of diligent service, if it neither asked nor bestowed the impalpable gifts of the less practical forms of daily benevolence.

BUT before my ship comes in, she must first go out. My ship was the stanch schooner " Ida Izette" (or, as we said, *Isit*, accenting the first syllable), and she was built in Waterside and launched beside the little wharf of that hamlet.

Waterside was a delicious little nook of virgin rusticity, sweet with the breath of clover meadows, and salt with the wholesome savor of the bay. Nestled on a gently sloping shore, it was sheltered by its curving, sickle-shaped beach, and it looked meekly up to the faint outline of Mount Faith, blue as a cloud in the distance. Its narrow, turfy " laneways," its moist fields, where fringed gentian may be abundantly gathered, or its sandy " driftways" made for the uses of the " seaweed privilege," are still quieter now than they were twenty-five years ago, when a boat-building industry peopled the village, with captains and carpenters. These classes were the owners of the thrifty little shops, savory with fresh odors of newly planed pine, and luxurious with piles of long, rustling shavings, covering the floor ankle-deep; and of the trim cottages embellished with rustic work, and graced with tokens of pains-taking taste and sea-faring bounty, in the sweet-brier by the window, or the pink-lined shells in the porch. To-day one of these dwellings, made fine with bay-windows and piazzas that are dotted with hammocks and camp-chairs, and provided with a carefully mounted telescope, is but the summer tenant's ornate reproduction of the native's snug habitation; which showed only such unstudied signs of local color as the spy-glass kept on the hooks of the cleat in the kitchen, or a half-hemmed sail thrown on the rag carpet of the " front-room," and awaiting the afternoon leisure of the daughter of the house, — " Cap'n Bill's 'Liza," or " Cap'n 'Lijah's Emmeline; " for in this compact, homogeneous, and kindred community, to designate house-holders and their families by their surnames would have been to use a superfluity of sound.

The launching of the " Ida Izette " was a long-anticipated event that brought together with one accord the dwellers in Waterside and its neighborhood, as well as certain representatives of that gypsy class not then known to us under the curt term of " tramps," but more feelingly described by the half-patriarchal appellation of " old travellers."

Among those witnesses of the ceremony who might be called its patrons was an amiable old

gentleman, the latest descendant of a family
once numbered in the Narragansett squirarchy,
but which had wasted its possessions with the
facility of the improvident Irish gentry. This
bachelor squireen, then, who bore the hereditary
name of Silvanus, was a gentleman of small
estate, but large leisure. Reputed " not so wise
as some folks be," his education, both early and
late, had been of a desultory character. But he
was an untiring reader, fond of historical dis-
quisitions, especially attracted by the fortunes
of the Ptolemies, and imperilling the gravity of
his listeners by invariably styling them the
"Pottlcomies." An instance of the inevitable
devotion of the gentle Squire Silvanus to any
utterly unpractical interest, and the fine indifference with which he met any worldly crisis, was
related by neighbors who dwelt upon the palmy
days of the Squire's middle life, and the afflu-
ence with which he was no longer burdened.
Narragansett was still famous for its dairy
products in those days, and a packet-sloop
lying at the Northeast Ferry was to be loaded
with cheeses from the Cape Farm, with other
shipments of the country trade. The wind was
fair for departure, but this particular share of
the freight was delayed, until the Captain himself, impatient to weigh anchor, went to inquire
of the tardy Squire. Nobody at the farm could
tell where the master of the house was to be

found, but the Captain, muttering wrath, strode
heavily on through the wide, bare rooms of the
old house until at last the rickety garret-stairs
groaned beneath his masterful tread; and there,
in a dusty, cobwebby corner, was the spare, bent
figure of the Squire, crouched in the characteristic attitude which had gained him the sobriquet of "Scrunch-up," and eagerly peering
through the pebble glasses of his heavy silver-
bowed spectacles at the yellow pages spread
before him. Happily oblivious of all homely
cares, Silvanus was busy with the congenial
labor of polishing his pedigree. Strewn around
him were letters and family papers, and piled
beside him were the old volumes of divinity
reserved for his recreation in reading when his
antiquarian toils should be suspended. "Bless
my soul, Zach! I forgot all about it!" was the
only explanation that could be drawn from the
innocent student by the irate man of affairs; and
after indulging in some of the polite language
cultivated by men of his·calling — perhaps no
strange sound to those walls "if ancient tales
speak true," nor wrong the reputation of their
founder, known as "Wicked Will" — the Captain turned his back upon the meek descendant
of that fiery ancestor, and left the Squire to
solace himself with further researches in the
buried treasures of the garret.

The greatest contrast to the kindly Squire in

all the company was old Grinman, the capitalist
of the place, as much envied as the *richard* of a
French village, and known as the hardest man
and the worst neighbor in the district. Misan-
thrope and miser, his presence at the little
gathering was but a matter of accident, and was
no sign of sympathy with the interests of his
neighbors.   He was almost a sorcerer in the
village opinion, in virtue of his reputed wealth
in bank stock, and his recondite attainments in
ciphering, — anecdotes of his profound skill
in figures being in part the foundation for the
awe in which he was held.   He had a long
head, as was commonly said of him, and, yes,
he had good headpiece, the villagers assented,
but he was a nigh-dweller, and no neighbor, as
poor Widow Broomer declared, when he lamed
her cow by stoning the creature out of his
pasture. Age had not humanized him, or made
him tolerant of his kind, and as he stood apart
from the crowd surveying its bustle with a sneer,
his cold and cruel eyes dealt stabs of quite
another character than those described by
Mercutio.

The well-to-do farmer of the community, and
one of the principal shareholders in the "Ida
Izette" was Sam D., who was always thus designated to distinguish him from the three or
four relatives who bore the same name and
patronymic.   The initial stood for nothing, hav-

ing been adopted when his business life began simply as a trade-mark by which the owner might be known. Sam D. was a shrewd, thrifty, bustling son of gain. He might be described as the realization of Yankee sharpness, mitigated by vanity. This always amiable trait modified the rigorous outlines of a nature hardened by early contact with toil and privation. He was the great man at all the funerals of the district, and would cheerfully lose half a day's work for the pleasure of burying an old neighbor. He pinched and saved, scraped and delved, lived on pork and porridge, with his hired men, and was, as they said, "clost as the bark to a tree;" then, with a delightfully childish prodigality, he adorned his wife with a gold watch, apparently for the sake of the satisfaction it afforded him, at the next funeral, to walk complacently through a room conspicuously furnished with a loud-ticking eight-day clock, in order to inquire in the general hearing, "Ma, what time is it by your watch?" With such occasional lapses into inconsequent expenditure and funereal geniality, he was but a neophyte in that stern worship of gain and scorn of humanity of which Old Grinman was so eminent an example; and the Yankee Timon regarded the busy, self-important, garrulous farmer with a sovereign contempt.

Among the pleasing instances of harmless

vanity in the rustic assembly was a queer, thin, piping, little old man, still wearing "the old-world corduroys," and dwelling long upon the advantageous advice, matured by long experience, he had given to the builders of the " Ida Izette." But he was never doubtful of his powers in any cause. It was a favorite hypothesis of his that if he could only have talked with " old King Gearge," the Revolution need never have occurred. His townsmen were disposed to find his local flights of fancy still more ambitious, as when he would wistfully ask, in his slow utterance: " Now, neighbor, what d' ye think makes Squire Potter and Squire Hazard always talk to me wheresumever they see me? " " Why, I don't know, Uncle Simon." " Well, neighbor, I 'll tell ye. 'T is to draar knalidge — yes, to draar knalidge." Simon was the happiest of men, and even dwelt mildly on his one grievance, the acquisition of an undesirable son-in-law, who was " a furriner from York," and was otherwise objectionable in South-County eyes.

Of course the chief mechanics of Waterside, and the builders of the schooner, Old Job and Young Job, were both present. Old Job was an immature patriarch of two score and ten, who held his brevet title of antiquity in right of a dazed, meek, Rip Van Winkle air, and because of the rapid and weedy growth of Young Job,

who had never overcome the shyness to which
he fell an early prey in the uneasy consciousness that his wits had hardly kept pace with his
stature. He was a most dutiful repetition of
his parent. Old Job was moderate, and Young
Job was irresolute; Old Job was plaintive, and
Young Job was querulous. Of griefs he had
an unfailing store, and he was darkly pessi-
mistic in his anticipations, especially as to the
mercantile fortunes of the "Ida Izette." He
weakly deplored the unwelcome presence of
old Grinman. Poor Young Job had never recovered from the shock which he received in
the sneer with which old Grinman once marked
his appearance on a Sunday in his best suit,
and accompanied by his wife and baby. Old
Grinman was no patron of the domestic virtues,
having long since driven his wretched family
into deserting the crazy shelter of his roof for
the charities of the world. The excessively
frail and feeble character of Young Job's constitution may be inferred from the fact that this
casting the evil eye upon him by Grinman so
overcame him that for the remainder of the
day he was obliged to rest on a rather unluxuri-
ous lounge of his own making. Young Job's
spouse was unfortunately another drooping
spirit, who did not seem to enjoy poor health,
though she said she did. She did not stand
high among her neighbors as an energetic

housewife. Indeed, Sally, our ancient help, used
to say that "nothing ailded Young Job but living on them dreadful stodges that Ann Frances
made." (A *stodge* in cookery is equivalent to
a *bodge* in handicraft.) It was, then, a feeble
hand that the youthful but infirm Job lent to the
work of launching.

Of course, the sad-faced womankind of the
village, dwelling in that shadow which seems
to brood perpetually over rustic matronhood,
lent their melancholy presence to the occasion. There were the Alzadys and the Celindys,
with plain Sarahs and Susans, and an irrepres-
sible mob of children, concerning whom their
plaintive mothers dejectedly exchanged con-
fidences; or held a conclave of agitated sunbonnets over the gossip suggested by the appearance of the usual pair of rustic lovers, never
absent from public gatherings, who walked hand
in hand with an Arcadian simplicity that was
quite undisturbed by the vociferous shouting
of their customary heralds, the group of derisive younger brothers and sisters who thus
proclaimed them: —

> "Ethan Streeter, see him ride,
> Sword and pistol by his side,
> And Hepsey Harvey to be his bride."

But nobody was annoyed by noise and confusion on this day of festivity, not even the

rather finical Clacksum girls, as the spinster sisters of that name had been known to Waterside for the last half-century. They had attained their three score and ten, and it seemed as if their late-lingering girlhood might in time give place to the estate of womanhood, with its titles and dignities.

No Waterside assembly was ever complete without the presence of the Elder, who was just at this time making one of his semi-annual visits to the hamlet. He was, as he often solemnly declared, "a wanderer upon the face of the airth," but he was not averse to a prolonged stay in comfortable quarters. He had scarcely reached middle life when, with a fine confidence in his species, he frankly threw himself upon the hospitalities of the countryside. His welcome, if not exactly enthusiastic, had been lasting, since he had journeyed from house to house in Narragansett for a generation. He came and went with the seasons; and his visits were as regular and inevitable as the intrusions of the professional tax-gatherer. The Elder's ministrations had been ungraciously declined by his sect, but he had now been for years, in virtue of his course of life, no inconsiderable preacher. His presence was in itself a sermon that enforced the duties of hospitality, and the graces of patience and toleration. It was worth while to help toward sustaining such a touching example of

trust in human indulgence, and such a convincing
instance of the occasional appearance in our hard
New England character of the simple traits of
the idle children of the South. Thus the Elder
might be said to be cultivated like some noble
exotic; and there was a genuinely tropical luxuriance and amplitude in his figure and bearing,
and in his florid vocabulary. On this occasion
he had exchanged a modest greeting with the
Squire, and sat not far from him, lost in drowsy
meditations.

The boys of Waterside found the impressive
presence of Gamby a stimulus to their faculties
of observation, and he was the animated centre
of a gaping crowd. Gamby was a stalwart negro,
a ward of the town-farm, and the massive iron
ball and chain which he dragged after him, and·
which was fastened to an iron band around his
ankle, was proof of the futility of the efforts of
his guardians to control his taste for roving.
With the brute strength of an idiot Samson,
and the instinctive cunning which lurked in his
admixture of Indian blood, he repeatedly made
his escape and roamed the country until he was
ready to return; for, though the common opinion was that Gamby did not know his strength, it
was noticeable that no one cared to test the truth
of this convenient theory. What with his shreds
and tatters, his half-running gait, and the sight of
his head rolling heavily from side to side, his

great animal tongue lolling out, and his glistening wolfish teeth all agrin, Gamby, in his useless fetters, was a spectacle that might have appalled a less easy-going community than Waterside. But the villagers regarded him stolidly enough, and to the children he was a highly acceptable realization of their ideal of a giant.

Another estray from the town-farm was Liz, a wretched old woman of shattered wits, who quartered herself upon her relatives in Waterside as often as she could evade the not very vigilant watch of her official protectors. After her tramp she would reach the village wrought up to the frenzy of a Bacchante by her desperate encounters with imaginary pursuers, and especially by the long abstinence from the healing leaves of that herb which she now begged of the crowd under the cry of " Backer! Backer! " It was told of this dehumanized object that she had been the handsomest girl of her time, and that a time incredibly recent, in view of the wild and haggard features that seemed never to have known youth.

Lettice Jetsam, a more commonplace vagrant, with no background of early romance to relieve her present uncomeliness, was searching the swamp on the Waterside shore always known as the " Indian Garden," whither, as traditionary story relates, Miantonomi resorted for the potent herbs used in his wigwam, pitched a few miles

inland, at " Miantonomi's Rock." With the aid
of her boon companion, a Charlestown squaw,
laden with baskets, her handiwork and stock in
trade, Lettice pursued her hunt after simples,
now and then addressing some shrill but unheeded admonition to her nameless imbecile
daughter, a gaunt and staring child of want,
whom Lettice had as yet failed to dispose of at
any of the houses where, after receiving charity,
she usually attempted to bestow her in adoption,
as a parting gift. This poor dwarfish creature,
huddled in her amorphous rags on a mossy
tussock, looked like some glowering gnome just
risen out of the earth. With her back to the
scene of the launching, which had no interest for
her, she stealthily repeated, with a gloating satisfaction, a series of signs and motions indicating the slaughter in a farm-yard to which she
had once been admitted when the sanguinary
artist in such work arrived, in order, as he ambi-
tiously said, to butcher the turkeys. This had
been the only scene of object-teaching that had
ever touched a responsive chord in her gentle
breast.

The decisive moment of the launching came
as a surprise at last; and the universal thrill that
responded to the lovely sight of the gliding,
white-winged thing of life, cleaving the sunny
waters that met her with a manifold welcome,
found expression in —

"The shout, prolonged and loud,
That rose from the assembled crowd."

The Squireen, standing on a little knoll,
waved his hand in benevolent patronage. Old
Grinman, the only unmoved witness of the emotion that pulsed around him, contorted his sar-
donic features in " a contemchous sneer," of
which Young Job feebly complained. Ann
Frances, Job's wife, who enjoyed a social dis-
tinction that was chiefly based upon the recondite character of the ailments that she cultivated,
was heard plaintively announcing that she must
go home right away, for she " had hild in her
breath so long, waiting 'round there, that she
was all nerved up, and she believed one of them
distressed spells was coming on." The cheering
was prolonged by Calvin Luther, the heir of the
house of Old and Young Job, who, whirling the
shattered straw hat that imperfectly thatched his
wildly straying locks, uttered a shout in which
he was ably seconded by his shrill-lunged sister,
Hannah Ann, who had deserted her patchwork
task and the company of her rag-doll, having,
in the words of her melancholy mother, " set up
a tease to come." The barking of the village
mongrels echoed this final hurrah and announced
the arrival of Joe Timmel, the singing stroller
of the Narragansett shore, and the itinerant
missionary of Calvinism. As the familiar figure
of the South-County Joe o' Bedlam advanced,

with his rolling gait, and his customary innocent
leer, the refrain of his favorite medley was
heard, "When the wicked am all burnt up —
ah!" and to the music of this benediction the
"Ida Izette" sailed down the bay. Its parting
echoes were still sounding as the little company
rapidly dispersed. The short period of cohesion
in the village community was over, and its atoms
were instantly scattered, each to its own place;
sympathy and interest had had their hour, and
idiosyncrasies resumed their rule. Only a small
group of shareholders and seafarers remained to
discuss the prospects of the schooner. Her
voyage was thus auspiciously begun in the pre-
lude of her successful launching.

> " Yon bright bark goes
> Where traffic blows,
> From lands of sun to lands of snows.
> This happier one,
> Its course is run,
> From lands of snows to lands of sun."

Such was the fortune of the " Ida Izette; " and
after a successful voyage, she made a pros-
perous run homeward, laden with a rich and
picturesque cargo. Her arrival was the signal
for a flocking of Waterside characters to the
wharf to share in the spoil. For days together
the hamlet wore an air of abandon and revelry,
while the welcome task of unlading went cheerfully on. Many a burst of rustic wit was hailed

with the ready laughter of open-air workers;
and the riotous influences of the scene penetrated even to the domestic interiors where the
children, feasting on the moist brown Mexican
sugar, had arrived at a state of ecstatic bliss,
and a quality of personal appearance to which
no expressions could do justice save the rugged
vernacular of their grandames, who announced
that it was " mux and gawm, gawm and mux,
with them childern, and wuss than a Sabbath
school picnic all the time." Waterside exulted
in the luxuriance of its tropical wealth. The
fragrance of the orange and the banana floated
on every breeze, while coffee and spices soothed
the soul of the housewife, and age was placated by the gift of a Tonka bean to enrich the
last supply of rappee. The village had indeed

> "Suffered a sea-change,
> Into something rich and strange."

Bright stuffs fluttered from the shoulders of its
damsels, gay bunting draped its porches, and a
new and splendid fauna had suddenly appeared,
as though the schooner had been a complete
Noah's ark. Paroquets fed tamely with pigeons,
and great macaws sunned their gaudy barbaric
plumage, looking like Indians in war paint.
Dearest to the heart of boyhood was the caged
"wildcat" still held in quarantine. He was a
small, fierce, black, restless creature, not easily

classified by means of the most diligent study of
the press and plates of "Goldsmith's Animated
Nature," but ravenous to a charm, and devour-
ing red, raw morsels with the insatiate appetite
of a Ugolino.

Time would fail me to tell of all the wonders
of sea and shore which gladdened the eyes of
Waterside dwellers, at the advent of the good
schooner "Ida Izette." But memory has laid up
in store the fragrant associations of a time when
our little strip of New England coast basked in
the borrowed atmosphere of the tropics. We
children all went to the most delightful of
schools in making acquaintance with the deck
and the hold of the "Ida Izette;" and such
were the treasures we found in those charmed
regions, so rich are the recollections of this
choice episode in our child-life, that not one
of us all can be so ungrateful to our kindly fates
as to deny that once, at least, to each of us, our
ship came in from sea.

THE wayfarer in the South County of nearly forty years ago might find himself, like Dante at the beginning of his pilgrimage, before the entrance to a dense wood. With its goodly oaks of a century's growth it looked a forest primeval. But it was, according to the tradition of the countryside, the plantation of a choleric old squire, who, in his resentment at finding himself cheated in a bargain for cordwood made with a shrewd neighbor, swore roundly that no heir of his estate should ever suffer a like annoyance; and immediately planted the sandy plain sloping to the river that bounded his patrimonial acres with oaks and maples, and had them cultivated by his negro servants, until they had well begun that growth which now in its maturity overhung with shade the smoothly sloping banks of the stream of the full-syllabled Indian name, the accepted meaning of which was in keeping with the practical tendencies of the aboriginal mind, for it signified " plenty of fish." Thus by the kindly offices of Nature the wrath of man was turned to praise; and the plantation which perhaps originated in caprice or anger, but was doubtless continued from worthier motives, kept green the memory of the bluff old squire.

Following the cart-path which led through the wood to the water, the pilgrim was from time to time met by creatures as strange and nondescript as any that were encountered by the observant Gulliver in his adventurous travels. Long-legged and awkward, with sodden elf-locks, shrunken features, abject and cowering air, and frightened cry, the silly sheep — as the poetry of old English rustic life, with Homeric persistency of epithet, constantly styles them — rushed by, shivering from their involuntary plunge in the cool waters of Rocky River.

The principal sheep-washer, who was suddenly discovered as a turn in the path brought the scene of the day's labors into view, proved to be a shepherd of souls as well as of sheep. He was no other than the powerful exhorter, Elder Bissell, or " Bizzle," as his name was currently known. Tall and muscular, though bony, stooping, and ungainly, his lank black hair, high cheek bones, inky eyes, and swart complexion, presented a suggestion of that reversion to the aboriginal type which is so anxiously sought by fanciful ethnologists. The Elder was a daily laborer on the farm, as well as in the spiritual vineyard, and might well sing with particular fervor of

> " Flocks that whiten all the fields
> All the stores the garding yields."

Just now, as he took the mute but struggling sheep brought from the pen by the waterside in the firm grasp of Benjy, the sinewy youth who waded out to him as he stood in the stream ready to plunge his panting prey under the current, his action inevitably suggested those kindred offices which he often rendered in the same surroundings to his human flock who sought in Rocky River the blessings of Jordan. The Elder's ministrations were naturally charged with the ghostly influences of his native region. The Dark Plains, as they were strangely called, perhaps from their lack of spiritual enlightenment, had from ancient times been the walking-ground of "harnts," the centre of witchcraft wonders, and even the scene of meetings with mysterious beasts and talking birds, whose intelligence, as described by the belated traveller who had heard and seen them on his tardy return from the husking frolic, suggested the keenness of their prototypes of an "Arabian Nights'" story. One of these raconteurs used to relate the story of his tarry at an apple-bee, at which the vintage of the last year's cider-press had flowed a little too freely, and of his homeward return by a path which crooked and turned unaccountably, but in which he constantly met, when crossing the Plains, a very knowing little bird, who hopped by his side with the persistent reproach, "Oh, Tom, Tom, how could you, Tom!"

These tales of the Plains often found a narrator in the sheep-washer who was the Elder's co-laborer, and who on more favorable occasions than the present would impart this ghostly lore to the circle that met at the same spot on Rocky River for the winter pursuits of the eel or smelt-fishing. The struggle with the affrighted subjects of his treatment now required all his attention, and drew rather heavily upon his patience; for his proper calling was that of a shearer, and he was serving in a humbler capacity merely to oblige his friend the Elder. His great display of skill would be made on his return, a week later, to shear the sheep that were now turned loose as fast as they were washed. Each helpless creature, seized in a tenacious grasp, would be speedily routed, as it were, from its fleecy shelter. The unrelenting shears would run with practised skill under the woolly locks, severing the clinging mass, which the deft touch of the worker rapidly rolled up into the fleece of commerce, as easefully as the mower sweeps down the swaths when the grass is wet with

falling rain. Thus denuded of its coat, the
animal stands forth in all the rugged harsh-
ness of its bare framework, and is discovered
to be but a scaffolding for sustaining a load
of wool. These living results of the shearer's
handiwork vie in precision of ugliness with the
grotesque achievements of the artisan in wood-
carving.

Nor were admiring witnesses wanting to the
skill of those masters of muscle, Elder Bizzle
and Uncle Shearman. Besides Benjy, the abler
of the two attendant youths whose presence was
indispensable to the success of the work, there
was the usual knot of idlers without whose
countenance no special episode of rustic labor
is ever completed. They are always ready to
assist by their attendance, and will kindly give
character to any of the undertakings of their
neighbors, however remotely they might be
supposed to be interested in them. So, like a
Greek chorus, which laments, but never rescues,
the spectators loudly ejaculated "Whew!" or
"Jericho!" at sundry crises in the washing,
as when Benjy, the chief acolyte of the ceremony, missed his footing on the pebbly bank,
and nearly lost his fleecy burden; but gave no
sign of leaving their more or less easy perches
on the stone-wall bounding the wood-lot, to
come to his help.

But now the noon-spell arrived, with its tacit

summons to the mid-day meal, and the attendant chorus gave tokens of a lively sympathy
with that phase of the day's proceedings. The
laborers sought each for his own ample portion,
brought that morning from home, and fell to
with a will upon such cold viands as boiled
pork and greens, johnny-cake and pickles,
"white bread," pie, and gingerbread. These
combinations were discussed with a vigor too
often wanting in these degenerate days, in
which even the Old Farmer's Almanac of this
current year recognizes the existence of nervous
prostration.

Among the "raft" of loungers, as the Elder,
with pardonable surliness, styled them, and who
now joined the group at dinner, was that always
entertaining itinerant, "Doctor" Billy Hood,
who was not slow to claim the brotherhood of
man, and especially of doctors, but recognized
no other remedy than his own specific, the
"Compound Tar-Water," the virtues of which
he extolled in the pauses of the meal. Another
aged stroller and vender of simples, was the
supposed possessor of certain occult powers of
healing, drawn from an hereditary source. The
local records were reticent as to the origin of
Gamper Boose; but local gossip derived it from
a not very remote Indian descent, a belief which
naturally gave great currency to his herbal re-
cipes. This "relic of barbarism" was seated

by another survivor of his generation, "Major"
by name. If he had ever borne any other, he
had lost it somewhere in the course of his
Wandering Jew existence; but he was said to
have earned his present sobriquet by having
"old-sogered it"—that is, shirked and scamped
his work—on the few occasions when he had
been numbered among the "work-folks" of a
farm. Spoken of as being "a little off, you
know," he excited no surprise by his minute
and fluent accounts of the injuries he suffered
from the witches who made him their nag,
riding him to and from their nightly meetings,
meanwhile leaving him tied to a tree, which he
could readily identify the next morning. Thus
grievously tormented by night, he groaned by
day under the dire results of this weird ma-
lignity, with as many stitches and rheumatic
cramps as Caliban foretold to the clowns who
provoked the revenge of his master. Now this
venerable man, having "come down to us from
a former generation," was sometimes unex-
pectedly exacting in clamoring for a return to
the wholesome and laudable usages that obtained in his youth,—as when he puzzled the
farmer's daughter, who had served his dinner
in a tin plate, by demanding (in the spirit of
the Roman lyrist forbidding a Persian luxury
of attendance), "Gal, hain't you no trencher?"
and after meeting the handmaid's vacant look

by a snort of disgust which fairly made her jump, he sternly pronounced, with manly independence, " Then gimme a *chip !* " — which service was meekly rendered.

The talk which seasoned the meal ran upon topics no less vivid than religion and politics, — the conversational staples of less effete circles than such as weakly exclude these firebrands of debate. The prospects of the national parties were freely handled ; but with the usual tendency of the contemplative rural mind to revert to pensive meditation upon the past, the glorious memory of the immortal log-cabin campaign, with its abundant flow of hard cider, was invoked by that element of the company which had long been known to the manipulators of local elections as a doubtful quantity, and liable to be diverted to this side or the other by certain quite irrelevant causes. The transition from teetotal principles to religious speculations was readily made, and the group was soon engaging the question tentatively propounded by the philosophical Doctor Billy, " How do you take the Bible? " Various replies were promptly chorused, as " I take it promiscuously," or " I take the Good Book by and large ; " but the Elder, waiving his prestige as spokesman, suavely sought to entrap his neighbor in the toils of doubtful disputations, by repeating in slow and ponderous tones, " Brother Shearman, how do you take it? The good word is with you, sir."

" Well, sir," replied Brother Shearman with masterly strategy, " I take the Bible literally, as you may say, from Amen to Genesis."

The momentary pause which succeeded to the assumption of this impregnably orthodox position was suddenly filled by the sound of voices from the river, singing in high feminine tones, and with fervent emphasis, —

" Oh, *brother*, ain't you g-l-a-a-d you 've *got* your *soul converted ?*
Oh, *sister*, ain't you g-l-a-d you 've *got* your *soul converted ?* "

" That 's Grandmammy Harley to a T," remarked Doctor Billy Hood with an evident air of patronage ; while Elder Bizzle's brow clouded with a sternness which could imply nothing less serious than doctrinal disapproval.

The rather battered craft that presently rounded the wooded point of land which had covered its approach was seen to contain the chief singer, a woman of imposing amplitude of figure and a tempest-tossed countenance, turbaned and barefooted, but vigorously keeping time with feet and hands to " her voice's music," as Sidney says of his young Arcadian shepherdess ; while another elderly woman, gaunt and cynical of aspect, yet with some suggestion of a Yankee Ophelia in a certain disorder of

.4

dress, joined in occasionally, as she rowed with
a stern and aggressive action; and with them
was a delicate girl of sixteen, who panted at
the effort of bailing out the leaky boat, as she
mingled her sweeter notes with the devotional
outcries of her grandam.

Grandmammy Harley was in the full fervor
of the very last of her campmeeting conversions.
She had experienced several of them, but was
a quiet and harmless soul in the intervals.
When not playing the Pythoness under the
stimulus of some itinerant Millerite's exhortations, or when, as she more picturesquely described herself, she had again become " a cold
and backslidin' perfessor," she made a steady
and efficient farm helper on such occasions as
soap-boiling, or "killing," or as cook in the stress
of haying-time; for she was skilled in the whole
duty of woman respecting pies, pickles, and pre-
serves, having been brought up at a country
tavern that was managed in the old-fashioned,
easy-going, free-handed way; and she was not
backward in tendering advice when present at
the celebration of kitchen mysteries. " An nef
I was you, Mis' Hahzard," she would be moved
to say, in the deliberative speech of her merely
work-a-day phase of being, " I 'd chuck in the
t' other handful o' salt.   Salt ain't dreadful salt
this year," she would add, with a reflective air.

Her daughter, the tall spinster, who looked as

old as herself, and who was invariably addressed
in her native community, with a particularity
that savored of Russian ceremony, by her full
title of Olive Ida Ann, had at some remote
time passed through an experience indefinitely
described by the tongue of neighborhood gossip
as being " crossed in love," — a saving clause
which was always charitably recalled in excuse for
habits and notions that were, as the same privileged tongue proclaimed, "queer as crazy Jane."
A fanciful observer might have found in her
name no fortuitous concourse of syllabic atoms,
but a prophecy of the different phases of her
nature and experience. " Olive " stood for the
exotic tastes and traits that appeared in her
flagrant eccentricities, " Ida " was a reminder of
such girlish graces as her youth had been dowered withal, and " Ann" represented the long
work-a-day stretch of her years, the dull drudg-
eries of her life, and its deadly monotony of
routine. Perhaps it is partly in an unconscious
need of change, if only from the kitchen to the
sick-room, and in the supreme feminine desire
of managing and ordering, that so many women
of her type and condition are so zealous in the
neighborly offices of nursing, house-keeping, and
general usefulness. Olive Ida Ann's energies
were appreciated among her afflicted acquaintances, and despite her well-known oddities and
rather unconscionable requirements, she was at

home wherever there was suffering; or, as she
more vigorously expressed it, she "could n't set
still waiting for the skies to rain porridge, when
there was folks to be done for." Not content
with serving her convalescent patients, she knew
no shrinking from those last offices which remained to be rendered to such as had passed
beyond hope of recall to human activities. Her
muscular arms and toil-marked hands were so
closely associated with the grim services which
she tendered almost too readily, and to which
she referred with the rugged freedom of her
class, as to make her presence such an oppressive *memento mori* as sufficed to dash the spirits
of weakly sensitive people. Why is it that the
same conditions that form the background of
the refined and picturesque figure of the Sister
of Charity are so obtrusive when viewed as the
surroundings of the untrained, unrecognized
Yankee nurse and village Samaritan? Perhaps
the clothes-philosophy may afford a hint towards
the solution of this minor problem; and possibly the daughter of Rome owes to her veil and
scapulary that halo of sentiment which fails to
grace our worthy neighbor's sunbonnet and
apron. Olive Ida Ann's surplus activities
were expended upon flowers, for which she had
a positive devotion, and she toiled at unseason-
able hours of dawn and twilight among the beds
of scarlet lychnis, sweet-william, and mullein

pink, that brightened her beloved garden. The
figure of the maiden gardener, herself the fair-
est flower, is one that cannot be spared from
poetry; but mistaken would be that observer of
actual rustic life who should credit the daugh-
ters of a village with any large share in the development of its floral attractions. These lovely
young persons are far too much occupied with
adornments of a strictly personal character to
consider the lilies of the field or the garden.
No, it is almost invariably the old and trembling grandam, the middle-aged widow, or the
ancient spinster, who dedicates herself to the
service of nature and the worship of beauty, —
though these fine phrases do a manifest injustice
to the loving simplicity of their maternal nurture of those childlike creatures, the flowers.
Olive Ida Ann was an adept in wood-lore, and
she had in charge the baskets which were to be
filled with sassafras, and other woodland growths,
for the brewing of the root-and-herb beer, and
the concoction of the bitter tonic drink intended for the use of the orphaned sick girl,
Ad'*line*, as she was known to her grandmother
and aunt.

Ad'line had possessed her full share of that
delicate prettiness which in many village girls
reaches its brightest bloom at fifteen or sixteen;
and even now, in the gentle decline which, su-
perinduced by a fever, advanced so impercep-

tibly as to be mistaken by herself and her
friends for a tedious convalescence, or, as they
said, "a real poor getting up," the pure tones
of the touching paleness of her face — its slightly
accentuated outlines softened by the mass of
rich, dark-red curls, of a solid roundness, like
the heavy ringlets treated with such realistic
care in Assyrian reliefs — were not without the
lingering charm of a vitality which still reigned
in the lustre and coloring of the hair and the
wine-dark eyes. Among her associates and
occasional schoolmates, like Benjy, the well-
made and frank-faced youth who acted as the
Elder's helper, no disappointment was felt at
Ad'line's immobility of feature, for they all
shared the same rustic fixity of expression.
Said an observer, who was piqued as a man
and baffled as an artist by the "freezing gravity" of a Greek princess whose portrait he
painted at Constantinople, "Her small mouth
and deep-colored lips might be embellished with
smiles, but I never had the pleasure to see
them." Now Ad'line, without being a subject
for the restrictions of court etiquette, was yet
not unlike this haughty beauty, for smiles she
had none. Her laughter was ready enough when
anything seemed funny, but the angel of smiles
and dimples had never troubled the waters of
her serene young soul. She had played for a
brief childish hour in the shallows of existence,

and she was soon to go down in the deep waters of death without ever having known the meaning of life. But no shadow of this darkening fate touched her with any sense of the adverse that appeared in voice or manner. She showed only that slight languor of illness that lends something of the repose of breeding to the most untaught, as she met her late schoolfellow with a frank "How d' do, Benjy." Her sweet gravity almost gave her the air of having said, "How does thee do?" like a maiden not of the world's people; and Benjy, who had been furtively brushing aside the crumbs of his repast, and spurring up his rather unpractised social powers, essayed to reply in tones that should be manly, but kindly, cheerful, and cordial, "How d' *do*, Ad'line? How *be* you?" But the result fell so far below his anticipations that without a word more he disappeared in the wood, whence he presently emerged bringing a vast armful of sassafras-saplings with the case of one of Milton's warlike young angels bearing his uprooted pine, and was quite satisfied that the object of this devotion accepted the offering with a mildly pleased expression that was equivalent to a smile.

"Ad'line," urged the now emboldened Benjy, "don't you want to ride a piece? I ben working on the jump all the forenoon, and I'll get Jakey to spell me while I go over and tackle up,

and I'll take you and your folks right up to
Broad Hill. There's roots enough up there."

"No, I cahn't, Benjy," returned Ad'line, un-
compromisingly. "Olive Ida Ann would n't
stir a step. She says she won't be beholden
to men folks for nothing."

"Good land!" ejaculated Benjy, with such
a foolish face of wonder at this declaration of
independence that Ad'line laughed aloud.

While this idyllic scene was in progress, Grandmammy had been challenging the Elder, her
long-time theological foe, to a passage-at-arms.
She had no sooner caught sight of that Attila of
the "no-souled Advents," as he sternly designated them, than her visage brightened for battle.
Planting her footsteps firmly on the bank, and
leaving to Olive Ida Ann the sole care of their
craft, she, not unlike a threatening ship-of-war
with fighting signals all set, bore down heavily
upon the group of feasters.

"So it was," she accosted them, a tremor of
emotion agitating her ample draperies, and with
a menacing wave of her substantial arm, "So it
was, even in the Gentile days, when the children
of wrath sat down to riot and carouse, and rose
up to play. And my arrant to you is, look out
for jedgment, for the day is to come."

"Well, if ever I heerd sich a lurry," announced
Brother Shearman, in an evident transport of disgust, but uttering his indignation in the sluggish

accents of the slow-moving, deliberative tillers of the soil; and "What mought be your mind, Elder, on them p'ints?" querulously begged Gamper Boose, thrown into a senile tremor by this portentous apparition, and involuntarily dipping his gingerbread into a quite unnecessary bath of molasses.

Neither of the opponents thus pitted at each other took any direct notice of these appeals; but Grandmammy continued, "I tell 'um," her rotund notes rising higher, "the Lord He's coming in power and glory, in heighth and mighth, to rend and to slay; and He'll shake the dry bones of you," she suddenly ended, with scorn expressed in every line of her ample proportions, and wheeling sharply upon the withered and sapless Elder, who tried to look as callous as possible under the consciousness of the stifled mirth among the younger of the company that bore involuntary testimony to the point of the personal application.

"No, Brother Shearman," observed the Elder bitterly, in a tone of unnecessary loudness, and with a labored air of ignoring his antagonist, at the same time rising, as a signal to resume work, "I don't feel no call to dispoot these here things with backsliders and women-folks."

An approving murmur rose among the Elder's followers, swelling to a confused noise of angry agitation, much like the threatening buzz of a

swarm, and strongly indicating the instant pro-
mulgation of an edict of banishment against
Grandmammy and her unpalatable doctrines.
The pseudo Hutchinson turned with dignity
to her silent supporter, Olive Ida Ann, — who,
with consummate indifference to the maternal
outpourings, had been all the time champing dry
twigs like a ruminating griffin, — and abruptly
issued her marching orders. "Ad'line!" called
her aunt in thin staccato tones, and the girl
obeyed, only once frankly turning to look back.
Benjy, if the glance were meant for him, knew
nothing of it, for he was just then facing the
river, as he went toward the Elder, every muscle
set to his task of carrying a particularly weighty
and cumbersome old sheep. But it may be that
he heard with some undefined pleasure the ring
of a girlish treble in the notes of pious song that
floated down to the workers from the retreating
trio, as they paused in their search for simples
on the breezy heights of the hill pasture, and
united in a burst of fervent hymnody : —

> " Oh ! we 'll have a shout in glory,
>   And the saints 'll mount the air."

A ILSE CONGDON, whose inappropriately musical name of Alice her neighbors, with intuitive recognition of her salient characteristics, invariably reduced to a curt monosyllable, was a quick-stepping woman, with snapping black eyes, and a tightly-set mouth. Nature's danger-signals, reading, "Ware the Shrew," might plainly be discerned in her face and mien. She was a scold and a housewife, as some of her fellow-creatures have been artists, — by the force of an irresistible, innate impulse.

There must be a place in the economy of nature for the vixen, no less than for the gad-fly. Such a restless, wiry, shrill, unflagging impersonation of steely energy as the indefatigable Ailse Congdon was needed in an untidy rustic community, careless about its gate-fastenings, and indifferent to the condition of its door-yards. She did a good work when she stung her neighbors into the better civilization of a more thorough neatness and order. She might indeed think that she did well to be angered at the habits of unthrift in the revolt from which her temper had been cankered. Born of a drunkard father and a weak-natured, inefficient mother, the sentiment of reverence was easily uprooted from the thin soil which her harsh nature supplied for its growth. Struggling all her life with the adverse conditions of an imperfect world of original sin and dust, of moths and rheumatics, of spring cleanings and fall fevers, what wonder if, having been, as she said, always in a pickle, she should partake of the tartness of her surroundings? "Father, he was a poor shoat," she would say with stern truthfulness, to Huldy Pawn, her bound girl from the town farm, "and mother had n't sca'ce ever any ambition. I never got no chance to what you 'll get here, and you oughter sing praise be to Canaan all your days to think you 've got a home with me, f'r if I live I 'll larn you something afore I git through with you."

Huldy Pawn received these and sundry more searching admonitions with a staring-eyed and wooden-jointed obedience which gave her the air of a Dutch doll. A foundling of no romantic antecedents, a waif cast upon the reluctant charities of the town, a helpless pawn on life's checker-board, it was her destiny to become the satellite of that ruling planet, Ailse Congdon. Poor Huldy was of feeble intellect, or, in the vernacular, she was "not all there,"—a phrase which concisely indicated the poverty of the

under-vitalized organization which confessed its
needs in the weak eyes, cold hands, and thin,
ash-colored hair of the weazen-faced handmaid,
whose sixteen years had dowered her but scantily with the graces of youth.

Ailse Congdon followed the trade of a tailor-
ess, — that calling to which the capable and
strong-minded woman who scorns the flimsy
avocations of dress-making and millinery naturally turns. Huldy kept the house, or, as Ailse
contemptuously said, " puttered 'round " in her
absences among her employers, but never developed a spark of independent spirit in consequence of these interruptions of surveillance.
The charitably-disposed often said that it was
clear goodness in Ailse Congdon, giving Huldy
her keep when she did n't need her no more
than a coach needs a fifth wheel; but others
were shrewdly inclined to believe that the reason why Ailse would n't let her go was because
of her love of domineering, or, as they said, she
wanted to have somebody under her thumb.
The condition of a ruler without a subject was a
point of bathos to which the mind of our energetic housewife had never descended.

The house in which these two women grew,
one into years, and the other into a sickly
maturity which more than kept pace with the
hale age of the elder, was the same humble
homestead that had been left in a rickety condi-

tion by that luckless wight, the drunken father of Ailse, who finally had the grace to get himself drowned from his fishing-boat. The patient thrift and care of long years had so reclaimed it that it remained in a state of partially arrested decay. The lean-to was a little too suggestive of a fall-down as it rested helplessly against the rough-hewn stone chimney, and the roof sank away between the gables as the heart of a man knocks at his ribs when speedy collapse threatens. But it was a very neat and habitable ruin, after all, as no one could doubt who knew the potent housewifery of its mistress. It stood half-cornerwise, with no particular reference to the road or anything else, in that quarter of the little home-lot which had been chosen as most convenient for digging a cellar. The hand-breadth of dooryard, though never adorned by shrub or flower, was always guiltless of litter, its short grass being fiercely swept, as it were in a rage of industry, by Ailse and Huldy, with the birch brooms brought to the door by the sullen lords of the Charlestown squaws, who, at other seasons, tramped with baskets which they were too prone to barter for New-England rum, returning safe to their reservation only by the favor of those merciful chances that wait on the gypsy train. No tree stood as comrade to the old square-hewn chimney, for the ancient willow had been condemned by Ailse, owing to an

inveterate habit of shedding its leaves ; and the
sentence pronounced upon it, in which the fine
old clump of incense-breathing box was in-
cluded, because anathematized by its owner as
saluting her nostrils with " a pizen smell," was
gloatingly executed by the occasional factotum
of the household, Izrul Barnes by name, farm-
laborer by calling, and tree-butcher by taste
and inclination.

Izrul really stood in a wholesome awe of his
energetic employer, though he affected a manly
independence when off the premises, asserting
with a large plurality of expression, that Ailse
Congdon mought skeer her Huldy Pawnses, but
she couldn't drive no Barneses. His relations
with the hand-maid were naturally more familiar,
and Huldy served as the irresponsive object of
those colloquial attentions which provoked
Ailse Congdon to many a sharp comment on
Izrul Barnes's long tongue.

"Say, Huldy, I've brung in y'r wood," he
announced from the shed, as a signal for that
damsel to appear, armed with turkey-wing and
dust-pan, to remove any traces of his footsteps ;
and while she was thus employed, and he busied
himself outside with the repair of a disabled
saw-horse, he attempted a little gossip about
Huldy's quondam pastor, the Elder of a meeting
to which she had been admitted in a heated revival season, her grim guardian merely observing

that "Huldy 'd be a worse fool than she took her for if she stayed with such a do-little set as them was. If they ever brought anything to pass, she never knowed it." In fact, Huldy, after once meeting with them "to break bread," retired from membership, alleging to Ailse Congdon that the loaf used in the sacred service was of so poor a quality as to cast discredit upon the occasion and the church.

"Say, Huldy," resumed the cheerful Izrul, in his invariable preliminary manner, "I carr'd a load o' wood down to Ponder Zeke's Corners las' week, 'n' I see Elder Springer a kitin' along the road."

He paused as Huldy made a vigorous dash at an intruding hen, which, from furtively tiptoeing about, broke into an affrighted flutter and cackle, as she fled before swift-handed justice.

"Berried his wife, y' know, three months ago come nex' Sa'a'd'y," continued Izrul, in a sly drawl. "The Elder, he looks ez chipper ez a crow-blackbird in plantin' time. Seems to be all took up 'ith visitin' his people. Tell ye what, Huldy, you better sprunt up, 'n' fly roun', 'n' wear y'r bettermost gownd all day. Look out fr what chance the' is, ye know, ez ole Marm Chaffell said to her blind gal."

"I don' want no Elder Springer," fretted the feeble-minded one, under a dim sense of something sinister in Izrul's cajoleries. "Folks say

you 'd better think o' gettin' married yourself,
Izrul."

" So I do, darter, so I do," returned old Izrul,
soothingly; " and every time I think on 't, I
think I won't," he pursued, ruminatively. .

" 'T ain't no such smart doings to get married," asserted Huldy, with confidence. " Ailse
Congdon, *she* ain't married."

" Wal, I sort o' thought she was onct," hinted
Izrul.

" 'T wan't none to speak on, anyway," tartly
returned the satellite, leaving the woodshed
with a fling.

But it was true that Ailse Congdon, though
always known by her maiden name, had a legal
right to bear that of Jim Castle, the young
woodsman to whom she had been united in her
girlhood by the local Justice of the Peace. Six
months of wedded warfare sufficed to convince
.the rather hasty and self-willed Jim, as his
bride explained, with what was pronounced a
callous indifference to " the speech of people,"
that " he guessed he 'd ruther stay with his own
folks, and she would n't lift a finger agin it."
Jim had failed to live up to the one great article
of religion which possessed the soul of Ailse
Congdon, and with which she had informed that
of her handmaid, that houses are the great, solemn, cardinal facts of life, the shrines on which
the oblation of human wills and energies must

5

be laid. Dress fills the aspirations of some
women, but it was the sterner ideal of housewifery that was all in all with Ailse Congdon.
As the fine lady in the "Bread Winners" is consoled in her widowhood by gaining the use of a
double amount of wardrobe-room for her summer and winter gowns, so Ailse Congdon looked
at her tidy, unlittered rooms, and thought that
Jim was a good riddance; "she did n't better
herself, noways, when she took him." Perhaps
she was not intentionally hard and severe, but
she was of so intensely practical and matter-of-
fact a nature, so incapable of the rudest form of
imaginative sympathy, that if not actually in-
human, she was certainly a little less than
human.

Jim's absence had not been prolonged many
months when he was killed by the fall of a tree
which he was cutting down. The newly-made
widow received the news with composure, simply saying to the messenger that "she always
told Jim he did n't have headpiece for that sorter
work, and that a tree would fall on him some
day, and ruin him." She duly attended the funeral, and observed to Huldy on her return, in a
spirit of relenting toward the departed, that "she
did n't wonder, come to see more of his folks,
that poor Jim was so head fo'most about everything. She should think, by the looks of things,
they 'd had a hull beef critter cut up, and sich

porridge as them was, she would n't set afore a
Turk."

Ailse Congdon reached an iron old age without ever having known serious illness; and when
death came, it was after a short and sharp course
of pneumonia, brought on by the rigid observance
of her usual rule of having no fire in the house
after the spring cleaning was done. As she
knitted and shivered in her icily clean keeping-
room one May evening, Death struck her in the
side with his dart, as in the engraving in the old
copy of the "Night Thoughts" which slept undisturbed, except to be dusted, with the half-dozen
other volumes which had descended to her, and
which she had been too thrifty to destroy. When
she rolled up her blue yarn stocking that night,
her life's work was done, and the useful hands
were to lie idle until they should be folded away
out of sight forever.

But their owner was not one to give up the
warfare of life in a tame and spiritless fashion.
From her sick-bed she could see into the kitchen,
and was still capable of scolding an hour by the
eight-day clock, if Huldy, in the flurry of her
spirits, hung the skimmer on the wrong nail.
The Elder, who came to ask her if she was prepared for a change, met with a vigorous retort
from the sick woman, who, raising herself on her
elbow the better to transfix the intruder with
her steely glance, informed him, "I'd have you

to know that we 're a very long-lived family, and
if you hain't nothing but that to say, you 'd better go back where you come from."

Her next visitor was Aunt Hepsey Dempsey,
a well-meaning old Quakeress, who always had
a mission to the dying. It was equivalent to a
death-warrant to see her grotesque little lame
figure, making its halting approach to your
bed-side. Sometimes the sick proved docile
enough under her ministrations, — as when she
piously inquired of an aged hewer of wood and
drawer of water, " Zeb, is thee ready to die and
go to heaven?" and the old negro with the
humility of his servile race faltered, " Ye-es,
Miss Hepsey, if so be as I can't do no better; "
thus voicing the unexpressed sentiment of many
excellent people who seem in marvellous little
haste to go to a place that is always well
spoken of. But when, in her usual formula,
she desired to know of Ailse Congdon, " Is thee
resigned to die?" her words were flung back
at her.

" Resigned to die ! " cried the poor soul,
with such panting breath as remained to her;
" d'you think, Friend Dempsey, that anybody
oughter be resigned to die with the sullar only
half cleaned and the back yard not cleared
up? "

The prudent benevolence of the neighborhood was much concerned in behalf of the

prospectively destitute Huldy, and, in view of
the fact that Ailse Congdon had neither chick
nor child of her own, she was urged to leave
the little homestead to her faithful help, rather
than to the relatives, among whom she had none
nearer than some half-cousins of the third degree, upon whom she had always looked with
an eye of disfavor. But now she turned to her
own, as so often happens at the last, was cyni-
cally disgusted with Huldy's tears and alarms,
and grumbled at leaving her all to town's poor
of uncertain parentage. The pressure upon her
was continued, however, until she finally gave
way, rather to the benumbing influence of
death's narcotics than to neighborly persuasion, and consented to sign the will ·prepared
for her by the ever-busy Squire Codgers, a
fussy, self-important little man, who by brevet
title and volunteer service was the neighborhood notary, and was in great request for making out your deed or drawing your will at much
cheaper rates than you could get it done by
the legal profession. Ailse Congdon had been
scornfully wont to describe this learned neighbor as "the lightest kind o' timber," but she
accepted his proffered offices with an unnatural
taciturnity, and never spoke again after his visit.
So, as has been said of another, the poor creature was mercifully chloroformed by the hand
of Nature into a better world, where she could

drink from healing fountains and feed on strange
fruits, with virtue to make her over, even to her
bones and marrow. No less radical a change
could work the miracle of creating a soul of
womanliness in the rugged nature of an Ailse
Congdon.

The funeral followed in due course, with the
arrival of the chief of the clan of cousins, deco-
rously summoned by the neighbors, who had
now no fear of his claims, though he was well-
known to have come sharp-set for the property.
In the language of his recital to an admiring
auditory in the grocery store of his native village,
on his return, he "went right slap to work, sir,
to overhaul things; " and he overhauled them to
such purpose that he found a flaw in the work
of the amateur lawyer, got the will set aside, ·
and took possession of "the estate and effects
of the deceased," as he complacently described
the lean-to homestead and its contents, including the scanty wardrobe, which he reserved for
the harpies of his family, excepting one of his
kinswoman's oldest gowns which " he did n't care
if Huldy Pawn had, being as he did n't hold her
responsible."

"It's allers bottom up'ards 'ith *my* dish
when 't rains porridge," wailed the poor creature, with a felicity of diction borrowed from
the vivid vocabulary of her life-companion;
and, " Huldy, I vow for 't! You *have* carr'd y'r

pigs to a poor market!" was Izrul Barnes's
sympathetic commentary upon the hard usage
of a fate which threw her upon the world just
when her infirm, or, as her late employer had
been wont to say, her "slack-twisted" constitution was failing under the stress of time. She
drifted about from house to house for a while,
finding no home where her subserviency would
be taken as an equivalent for board; for with
the displacement from her accustomed surroundings, her hand had quite lost its cunning
in the routine-work which she had accomplished
under the searching eye of her mistress. Losing her head entirely for the time, she tramped
about the country until neighborhood charity
would tolerate her no longer, and she had
become "chargeable to the town." To the
town-farm then, whence she came, she was
returned; and, upon being accepted as a town
charge, began to develop the mysterious vitality
of a pensioner, actually living to a great age,
in which she often made the immaculate housewifery of her early patroness the theme of her
praises.

"Ailse Congdon was a faculized woman,"
she would say, in regretful memory of her
kitchen. "She couldn't have things *flush*, but
she was one o' them that gits a livin' off'n a
rock. And when you come to neat! — why,
you mighter gone all over her house, and you

could n't took up a teaspoonful o' dirt. She never let a drop o' the cleanest water stan' a minute on her kitchen-floor; 'n' lawsey! how she uster keep scoldin' me, in my young days, and a tellin' me how that any woman that did n't keep a shine onto her teakittle had oughter be buried alive!"

With this fitting obituary we will suffer the shade of Ailse Congdon to pass.

AN AFTERNOON AT NEIGHBOR
NORTHUP'S.

NEIGHBOR NORTHUP'S gambrel-roofed, weather-beaten, wood-colored homestead of one story and a loft might almost have been mistaken for a deserted dwelling, so riotous was the profusion of catnip and other fat weeds that flourished in the waste places of the house-lot, and so tall were the door-yard grasses that nodded familiarly at the window of " the gret room," as the diminutive parlor was designated, — " great " being an adjective not of size, but of state. But a faintly-marked, grassy footpath led from the rickety front gate to the rough-hewn stone that lay at the "green 'fore-door," — that being the conventional color of a principal house door, — and a more frequented way ended at the kitchen entrance, where Neighbor Northup sat smoking a peaceable pipe, and lending a condescending ear to the gossip of her meek henchwoman, the Widow Bill B., as she was lucidly styled, to distinguish her from the equally bereaved Widow Bill D., of the same ultimate family name. The Widow Bill, who had arrived

at half-past two o'clock to spend the afternoon
and stay to tea, with many apologies for not being able to come early, was solacing herself, in
her feebler fashion, by an occasional resort to
her snuff-box; and both women knitted vigorously at stockings of homespun blue-dyed yarn.
That excellent person, the Widow, resembled
nothing so much as an ancient and battered doll.
The hand of time had dealt with her meaningless
features as cruelly as the equally ruthless hand
of childhood deals with its nursery puppets;
and the discolorations and indentations which
age had imprinted on her countenance, with the
sparse and lifeless locks that here and there
clung in patches to a head of unfeminine bald-
ness, gave her exactly the air of one of these
hapless victims.

Neighbor Northup was cast in a sterner mould,
and her ugliness was of a more picturesque
character. The strength of her gray eye, hawk
nose, firm-set mouth and square jaw remained
unimpaired by the ravages of years. Her face
was of one uniform tint of gypsy brown, and her
iron-gray hair, combed straight back, was tightly
fastened in a frankly minute knot. Her gown
of dark-blue calico suited well with the Zincali
associations of her lean, erect figure, and self-
reliant air.

Harty, Neighbor Northup's granddaughter,
stood at the ironing-table, her fresh young

features delicately flushed, as the light dews of labor just moistened her healthy white forehead, disturbing with tiny tangles the neatly-smoothed waves of rich brown hair.   Harty sang at her work with all the *élan* of the song-sparrow, repeating again and again the same ballad strain of " Mary of the Wild Moor."   Sweet-brier petals, borne on the light breeze, fluttered through the little window and drifted among the coarse white folds of the thin-worn old linen sheets spun by her great-grandmother, as Harty, in her clear, fresh tones, sang the dreary refrain, —

> " Oh ! 't was there Mary perished and died,
> From the winds that blew 'cross the wild moor ! "

No feeling for the contrast between wintry moor and sunny meadow, between the child of home and the daughter of shame, no sense of the rude passion and pathos of the song stirred in the sheltered nature of the girl and moved her to dwell thus upon its recital of the never-ending story of desertion, want, suffering, and death.   Happily too young in thought and experience to be reached by any echoes from the depths of life, the words were of no particular moment to her, but the tune was a pretty tune, like any other.   In the unconscious charm of her untouched simplicity, she was the Yankee counterpart of that English peasant maid of whom the peasant lover exclaims : —

"How gently rock yon poplars high
Against the reach of primrose sky,
  With heaven's pale candles stored !
She sees them all, sweet Lettice White !
I 'll ev'n go sit again to-night
  Beside her ironing-board ! "

But, though Harty may be a living poem, she
is destined never to know it; and the story of
her life and its surroundings is to be written by
fate in such plain prose as belongs to this narrative of one afternoon of home-life at Neighbor
Northup's.

"Harty 's ez chipper ez a conqueedle," commented Widow Bill B., "and thet 's a real harnsum toon she 's a-singin'."

"Hum-ha," debated Neighbor Northup, who
was of a firmer mind than ever to give assent
to anything; "Harty favors me in her v'ice;
old Prisbyter'an Priest Brown uster say my
v'ice was powerful strong. Reck'lect, Betsey,
up to Elder Burdickses woods' meetin', to the
Dark Corners, the' was a hime chune 't we sung
b' spells. I don' know 's I could justly turn it
now," mused the dame, with an unwonted access
of modesty, which was presently quite justified
by her execution of —

"O sisters, I want you, —
I want you, and I want you,
To wear the glit'rin' crown."

"I always liked the 'Good Old Way' myself; it lined off real handy," suggested her

crony, sending off the dame upon the strains
of, —

> "Ez I went down 'n the valley to pray,
> A-studyin' about this good old way,
> Ez I went *down* in the *valley* to *pray* — "

"Merciful George!" suddenly ejaculated the
self-interrupted singer, regarding with lowering
looks an advancing group of figures; and "Mer-
ci-ful George!" she repeated with deepening disgust, "ef thiar ain't my darter Skinner an' her
ran-dan o' young 'uns, come ter spend the arternoon, sure ez pizen."

"Deary me, neighbor," echoed the pliant
Widow, "deary me, comfort is all to an eend!"

Neighbor Northup was by no means the
doting grandam of conventional narrative.
She cherished no weak fondness for her de-
scendants, and as often as she heard of any
death among children was wont to express no
slight disgust in that it had not been that of
one of her grandchildren. This arraignment
of fate was not prompted by any personal antipathy to her young relatives, but by the hard
common-sense of the matter, as she viewed it, —
"Skinner being sich a poor coot, and him and
her with more children than they justly knowed
what to do with."

"Lovisy Ann Skinner!" was the stern salutation addressed by Neighbor Northup to her un-
looked-for guests; "of all possessed! What

brung ye here, with all them tribes o' Beelze-
bub? Did ye ride or travel?"

"Me an' the childun, we travelled a consider'ble spell," drawled the impassive and
apathetic Lovisy, dropping into a splint-bot-
tomed chair and fanning her stout person with
the almanac; "but to the last on it, Cap'n Sailforth, he come along in his lumber-wagon, 'n'
we rid with him 'beout tew mild."

"Abner Sailforth, hey?" wrathfully returned
her mother. "I wish 't he was in Flanders.
Hain't he got nothin' to do but go cartin' of you
round?   Must 'ha ben wuss off 'n common."

"Well, he was kind of oh-be-joyful," admitted
Lovisy.

"Cap'n Sailforth, he's got a jug in his wagon,"
innocently piped up the youthful Jonas Skinner,
and immediately fled, howling under the sting
of a smart slap inflicted by the red right arm of
his grandmother, with a long brown towel which
hung at hand, while the grandmaternal accents
bade him "quit scandalizing [that is, slandering]
of his neighbors and betters."

"Don't ye tech them curr'ns deown to the
garding!" shouted the dame after the boys, as
they disappeared with suspicious alacrity in that
direction; "ef ye do, I tell ye now, I'll make ye
feel cur'ous!"

Quiet being now restored, the Widow made
some deprecatory inquiries after the health of

Lovisy and the absent Skinner, while her indulgent parent smoked in contemptuous silence,
as the long-drawn recital of the physical woes
of the pair welled forth from Mrs. Skinner's
voluble lips. Mr. Skinner, it seemed, was suffering from a cold, and "though he clapped to
and took everything he could think on (he was
always a Bettyin' 'round in the cluset) he wa'n't
no better, an' she misdoubted he would n't be
'round very spry by hayin' time. He mought,
an' then agin he mought n't, but things looked
dubersome." She herself languished under an
ailment the symptoms of which were not of a
character to inspire much sympathy when made
the subject of complaint in July weather, and
were described as the state of being "all of a
trimble, with cold chills running up and down
the spine of her back." As for the maladies and
misfortunes of the children, they were related
with a wealth of detail that seemed as endless
as the blocks of the Job's Trouble patchwork-
quilt with which her fat fingers (armed with a
brass, open-topped thimble) were appropriately
busied.

The talk next turned upon the neighborhood news, being the unprecedented luck of
one Tad Hooper, who was currently reported
to have discovered a gold mine on his farm.
"Skinner, he said," related Lovisy, not unwilling to find herself the enthralling narrator of

the hour, " he said how Hiram Collins should say thet Tad Hooper told him hisself thet he see it croppin' outer them rocks, chunk arter chunk ! "

" Why, Aunt Lovisy," interrupted Harty, who was listening with an interest that worked no little detriment to her ironing, " I thought Tad Hooper did n't know nothin' ! "

" Toby sure, thet's the way on 't, child," eagerly assented the Widow, in full enjoyment of the marvel, " ' the wheel o' fortin dooz for to go round,' ez the childern's father uster say, an' ' ef ye have luck, little wit 'll do,' says the childern's father, says he. 'T is so, ain't it, neighbor ? " she pursued, deferentially appealing to her stern hostess for corroboration of the philosophical moralizings of the late Mr. Bill B.

" Humph," shortly returned that lady, with a vigorous puff at her pipe, while her subservient auditory waited humbly upon her words, " I disremember what Northup moughter hed ter say 'beout it," she began, with the ironic chuckle of one who was above the weakness of quoting any marital dictum, " but I c'n tell ye what's ez sure ez jedgment, an' thet is thet the' ain't no gold on Tad Hooper's farm, nor never will be, 'cept fool's gold ; an' thet's the long an' short on 't."

This debatable utterance of the oracle was received in a respectful silence only broken by the return of the brothers, who had fallen out by the way, and who hastened to pour into the maternal ear an exhaustive narrative of the manner in which Henry Clay and Thomas Dorr had come to blows, the results of which political conflict were apparent in torn jackets and tear-smeared faces.

"Lovisy, *be* ye goin' ter let them childern ride over y'r head?" vociferated the dame, rising to her feet. "You Tom Dorr, hush now, or I'll shet ye up f'r the rest o' y'r nat'ral life. Y'r ma 'n' Widder Bill B., they can't hear theirselves think."

"Never mind, gran'mother," coaxed Harty, who had finished her ironing, "I'll git Pesky Phillups's old boat, 'n' go up the pond, 'n' the boys c'n go, too."

"Goody! Goody!" roared her interesting companions, and "Joy go with ye!" sarcastically shouted the grandam, as they disappeared with their cousin, — the girls of the party being detained by her orders.

"Hain't ye got no stent for them great gals, Lovisy?" she queried severely. "But mebbe they was all on 'em borned with silver spoons inter their mouths."

"Le's try 'em in their book-larnin,' neighbor," pleaded the peace-loving Widow; and the Old Farmers' Almanac being laid before Miry, aged eleven, with an encouraging injunction to do her possibles, she managed, after sundry

6

admonitions from her grandmother not to read so like a mouse in the cheese, to convey to the company the following piece of wisdom: —

"Farm-ers att-end This-is-the-time-of-good h-u-s hush, — no, suthin' else, — hus-hus-ban-dry f'r plantin' y'r mangle-mangles ["mangle wuz-zles, I expect, dear," whispered the kindly old woman, but the wretched Miry justified her name by plunging deeper in] mangles worsteds — no, 't ain't that — f'r plantin' y'r mangled weasels."

"Shet up thet there book!" came in hollow tones of disgust from the grandmother; and the Widow hastily complied, but beckoned to her side the little Medora, to hear her con her alphabet, and attempted to start her aright by repeating with nodding suggestiveness, "A bus-tle A, B bustle B, C bustle C — " "What 's them 'ere?" lisped the bewildered babe; and Lovisy, with explosions of laughter, informed the Widow that the teacher "did n't learn them that way any more."

"Dearest heart!" ejaculated the flustered Widow, "no, I b'lieve they don't, come to think; but seems so it don't come nat'ral to say 'em no other way. Myrandy's childern, they hollered, when I told 'em ter say 'Quf bustle quf.' 'No, gran'ma, 't ain't *Quf*, it 's *Q!* ' — but law! I did n't charge my mind 'ith it."

The Widow's early instructions had evidently

been imparted at one of those dame schools
where, for lack of books, the alphabet was re-
cited to the children, and hummed over by
them, in the form of " A by itself, A," etc., with
the inevitable phonetic rendering.

But what succeeded in the Iliad of Neighbor
Northup's woes? Came the return of Harty
and the boys, flushed and jubilant; followed
the four o'clock supper, laid a trifle earlier than
usual, with prudent forethought for the timely
exodus of Lovisy and her tribe, in order to
reach their own domicile by " airly candlelight."
Sing, O Muse, of "them porridge" (always known,
in Narragansett, by this honorable plural), of
johnny-cake and cold boiled pork, of rye an'
Injun bread, of flour cake, of cold vegetables
left from dinner, and, for the children, thoughtfully interspersed with tender shredded bits of
pork-rind.   Sing, O heavenly goddess, the
wrath of Neighbor Northup when this delicacy
was declined by the youthful Valorius (named
from an imperfect recollection of Bunyan's immortal tale), as he forcibly rejected the offending
morsel with an explosive commentary of, " I
don't like it, ma; I don't, I don't! "

"Uhdone! " shouted the grandam, in the
colonial corruption of the imperative " Ha'
done, sir," of English comedy.   "Uhdone, I
say, 'n' don't you darst open y'r head agin, 'cept
ter put y'r vittles into 't, or I 'll *rise* upon ye! "

— the last clause enunciated in fearful accents.
Meanwhile Charlotte Ludovica, a scrawny, sal-
low damsel of ten, was furtively partaking of
her fourth cup of scalding hot tea, precociously
taken without "trimmings;" for her mother
approvingly said of Luddy Lotty, as she was
commonly called, that she had n't a sweet tooth
in her head.

Calmer moments followed, while Lovisy strove
for a diversion by plaintively inquiring of Harty
"ef she wa'n't most beat out with rowin'." "*She*
ain't rowed none!" chorused the young bar-
barians. "Joe Phillups come right out arter
her, 'n' went with us, 'n' he would n't let us row
none, nuther."

"Jest wanted ter show off," grumbled Henry
Clay, with precocious discernment.

"Yes," agreed the equally aggrieved Thomas
Dorr, "an' him an' Harty kep' up sich an everlastin' jabberin' 't they skeered the turkles off
when we was clus' up to the rock, 'n' we did n't
ketch none."

"Oho," exclaimed Grandmother Northup,
but this time with simulated wrath, while Harty
flushed a painful red, "hes thet fool feller ben
pokin' 'round agin? Harty, I sh'd thought
you 'd a killed him or cured him, this time."

Lovisy here observed, with that superior and
patronizing air of calm judgment which one
woman never fails to show respecting the tender

history of another, that she "s'posed Harty knowed her own business, but f'r her part she should n't wanter live with his folks, for old Marm Phillups was deef 's a beetle, 'n' Pesky was cracked by spells."

"Don't you fret y'r skull, Lovisy," elegantly admonished the triumphant grandmother. "Guess Harty 'll do ez well, when her time comes, ez any of her folks hes done afore her!"

The dame's high good humor mounted to the point of presenting to Lovisy, as she bestirred herself after supper with preparations for departure, a relic from her wardrobe, to be made over for use in her young family.

"It's a clever gownd yit, Lovisy," said the grandmother, smoothing it approvingly, "but, good land o' patience! your Sarah 'Liza 'd thrash it out 'tween Cubit's Hill an' Potter's Pond. Ef thet there was my gal, I'd keep her sewed up 'n tow-cloth."

Provided with this benefaction and with sundry other spoils, Lovisy and her train departed to rejoin the twins, who had been left at home in charge of the six-months-old baby, his mother placidly remarking that "she guessed Moses 'n' Aaron 'd pretty much giv' him up by now." Harty took some hasty but indispensable stitches in the garments of the over-energetic Jonas, while the Widow Bill B. snatched a furtive kiss from

the chubby Medora. The boys dashed off as
though set free from school, — "Poley," who,
deriving his name from the tyrant Corsican, was
naturally the moving spirit in savagery among
them, secretly gloating over the consciousness
that his grandmother's useful tabby at that moment lay nursing a lame paw in the potato patch,
whither she had been driven by the mischievous
stone that dealt the wound, and, with some
uneasy apprehensions of judgment yet to light
upon her persecutor, bursting defiantly into a
catch of folk-song that had been handed down
in the race of Skinners, —

> "Oh dear! oh dear! what shell I do
> I 've killed my daddy's keow;
> I won't tell him on it ter-day,
> But I 'll tell him ter-mor*row*, — "

while Neighbor Northup, not as yet fully aware
of the various ravages committed on her territory by these invaders, and placated by the
removal of a serious cause of irritation, unconsciously returned an antistrophe to their parting
song, as she gave a long puff of relief at her
after-supper pipe, and thoughtfully struck up
the refrain, —

> "Believin', we rej'ice
> Ter see the curse removed."

FROM HOUR TO HOUR IN THE COUNTRY STORE.

THE country store might not be a gem, but it was richly set, in a background of darkly-wooded hills steeply descending to the stream beside which it stood. Thus secluded in its surroundings of woodland loveliness, its visible relations to the world of trade were so few that at the vacant hours when the mail-carrier was not due, and no boat lay at the rude landing, it might almost have posed to the wandering artist as the storm-beaten, moss-grown cabin of an aged settler in the primitive Narragansett wilderness. But it dated from the Revolutionary period, and, as was then customary in the South County, it formed an integral part of a large, gambrel-roofed, shingle-sided, wood-colored farmhouse, — being attached at one end of that structure, with its independent entrance from the road sometimes closed by a half-door, and its door of communication with the domestic apartments always conveniently ajar. This rather torpid nerve-centre of the sluggish life of the outlying farms possessed vital attractions for the

customers of the past generation, who arrived at
their goal by ox-teams, or, in eccentric instances,
by driving that cautious and conservative steed
in harness, or else riding him after the fashion
of " old Shawmut's pioneer," the hermit Blackstone. But such as did not drive the patient
oxen under their names of old-country descent,
as " Duke and Darby," " Buck and Bright," or,
in the later nomenclature of patriotic independence, " Star and Stripe," and such as did not
urge the reluctant Dobbin in the creaking cart
or the slow-jogging wagon, came by the water-
ways which lent a grace to rustic travel ; or else,
in their own phrase, " footed it " on the driftways, or over the hard-beaten little paths that
led across-lots. So, by the winding ways of old
lanes that nourished tall blossoming weeds in
summer, and when " the frost was coming out of
the ground," were ironically described by indignant women-folk as being " in full bloom " with
a luxuriant depth of mud ; by the old roads of
scarce higher degree, guarded in sub-baronial
fashion by a gate at every farm, and keeping
the same leisurely twists and turns that were
imposed to suit the convenience of the colonial
proprietors ; by the dark waters of the haunted
Hawkho Pond ; by the loops and curves of Pond
Lily Brook or Indian Run, — they all met at the
same point, in search of their household supplies,
and to call for the weekly newspaper, the " New-

port *Marcury*" or the denominational journal,
with the infrequent letter from the daughter who
was learning a trade, or the son who was "stor-
ing it" in some New England town. It was the
neighborly duty of the storekeeping postmaster,
or of the droppers-in at the store, to make known
the arrival of letters; and the "pleas forrard"
generally scrawled in the corner of one of these
missives was literally obeyed. The addresses
were almost uniformly in masculine hands, — it
being the received tradition among the women-
folk that a presumably gossiping feminine epis-
tle would be officially slighted, if not utterly cast
aside, to make way for the business communica-
tions of the serious sex. Occasionally a rustic
postmaster failed to comply with all the unwrit-
ten regulations of neighborhood law, but righteous wrath overtook him.

"I never see no sech do-little coot ez thet
Jim Fones," was the angry comment of Uncle
B'riah Sanford, as on his way home from the
store he accosted a neighbor, who heard his
story with equal indignation. "He ain't what
I call very work-brittle. Look-a-here, now, I
jest got this here letter my darter Marcy's writ
me, an' it's ben a-layin' over thiar nigh upon
three weeks. I dono where his wits was," pursued Uncle B'riah, with a bitter smile of scorn
for the sterility of the official mind, "never to
tho't on Dely Helums, thet mustee gal. She

goes by the store mos' gin'ally when she goes
up 't the big house chorin' of a Sa'a'd'y. He
mighter ben on the lookout for her, an' 'a' sent it
to me, well 's not. Wal, I guess ef Gov'ment
was knowin' to 't we sh'd see a change, right
short off."

The interior of the store, as seen on a mild
and hazy afternoon of mid-autumn, presented
its usual display of "infinite riches in a little
room," so far as a teeming variety answers to
the idea of riches. The needs of man and
beast, as felt at the So and So Corners, could
be amply satisfied here, so that it was commonly remarked that Elder Nahum Holley, the
begging friar of the Baptist persuasion, whose
itineracy the good people of the countryside
had tolerated for a generation, used to sing
with peculiar fervor when lodged at the store,
and after partaking of a refreshment flatteringly
described by him as "a very promiscuous puddin'," an original hymn, of which the rather
singular refrain was: —

> " All my critter wants employed,
> All my hours of rest alloyed,
> All my needs air well supployed."

The gifts of the season, in fruits and vegetables of the homelier sorts, occasionally found
a place here, — not for sale, of course, for who
would be so absurd as to buy " green sass," of
which everybody could raise enough and to

spare? — but as signs of the skill of their pro-
ducers. It was a spontaneous exhibition of the
works of nature, an inchoate rural fair. Behind
the bar, as it had been in the old times when
strong waters were dispensed to all comers,
from the Tory Squire to Injun Moll, that inefficient factotum, the blameworthy Jim, was shell-
ing some beans, rather disparagingly described
by him as comprising "all nations," but chiefly
of the "hundud to one" variety. A woman and
a little girl just entering the store became the
objects of a leisurely observation on the part of
the usual knot of loungers, which, in its undisguised air of languid routine scrutiny, could
hardly be surpassed by the spent nonchalance
of the watering-place stare.

"Mis' Tift," as she was presently addressed,
was a stout, hearty woman, of whose age the
less said the better, but who might have been
anywhere from the middle regions of the forties
to that abrupt descent of life which is oddly
described as "risin' fifty." This exemplary
matron was evidently of my Lord Bacon's opinion that "Virtue is like a rich stone, best plain
set;" for her dress was marked by severity of
choice, and comprised a massive pair of rough
leather shoes, fashioned by a veteran cobbler
who still plied his trade from house to house, a
calico short-gown and petticoat, with a long
apron, and a log-cabin sunbonnet. She had

coarse, harsh hair, styled "molasses color" by
herself, and springing from the top of the forehead in that point which is esteemed a mark of
beauty, and of which one of the ladies of the
Stuart period makes a charmingly complacent
mention in her memoirs, when enumerating her
attractions.   But, treated as it is on rustic faces,
the effect is as decidedly ugly as is the meeting
of a pair of black eyebrows (which the Romans,
with characteristically bad taste, nevertheless
admired) ; and hence, perhaps, the invective
with which it is loaded in the vigorous bucolic
speech, — being known as "scold's peak," and
yet more derisively, as " a cowlick."

The child of ten who accompanied her was a
victim to the high-low cut of the dress of children at that day, by which the shoulders of
little girls were neither set free nor quite restrained, so that restless childhood was continually
thrusting up one shoulder or the other in the
revolt from the uneasy bounds which fretted
but did not confine.   Her tow-colored locks,
kept neither long nor short, were all gathered
in one "wisp," and tied with a bit of faded
ribbon, supplemented with a colored shoestring.
She was of an ill-nourished aspect, and bore the
large-eyed look of illness; or, as her mother
more graphically said, "she was as poor as a
crow, and her eyes were as big as saucers."

A faded, fussy, nervous little woman, who

had come in with a deprecating air, after fidget-
ing about for a few minutes, approached Mis'
Tift, who was volubly beating down the store-
keeper in his tariff of West India goods, and
addressed her with an apologetic 'hem, yet with
something of the modest assurance of one who
knew the proper forms of polite inquiry.

"I wanter know, ef 't ain't imperdent in me
ter ahsk, ef this here ain't Salome Stillman thet
was?"

"Well, I calc'late 't ain't nobody but the old
woman herself," graciously replied the owner of
this complex individuality, "but, my stars 'n'
garters, woman, who in time be you?"

"Why, Mis' Tift, don't you reck'lect Mis'
Crandall, Samwell Crandall's wife, she thet was
a Rose?" queried Jim Fones, perceiving that
the office of master of ceremonies devolved
upon him.

"F'r the land's sake alive!" exclaimed Mis'
Tift, as she rigidly scrutinized the faded and
withered features of her that was once a Rose.
"Why, Nabby, heow you'm broke! You'm
growed gray, an' you'm wrinkled some, an'
you'm bent over, an' y'r teeth's most all gone,
ain't they. Lor', I should n't ha' knowed ye
from Adam."

"Well, I expect I be changed some," returned the meek Mis' Crandall, evidently with
some slight twinge of the pain known to even

the most homespun woman on becoming a prey
to the attacks of ruthless time, " but I sh'd 'a'
knowed you agin, S'lome, ef I 'd 'a' met ye in a
porridge-dish.   And heow 's y'r heaalth, nowa-
days ? "

"Tol-lol, on'y jest tol-lol; jest so 's ter be
abeout," continued Mis' Tift, with increasing lu-
gubriousness.

"And heow 's little sissy?" pursued the sed-
ulous inquirer.

"Well, 'Mandy, she ain't a bit well.   I ben
mithered more 'n little ter know what ter do with
her.   Looks dretful poor in the face, don't she?
['Mandy falls into a state of wriggling self-consciousness.] 'Pears ter me she's kinder consump-
tive. (Take y'r shoulder in, 'Mandy, that ain't
pretty.) I ben doct'rin her, back along, with
some o' these boughten pills, but they come
oration high,— thutty-fife cents f'r the *big* box,
— so 't I gin 'em up, an' I 've kep' her on yarb
tea now, stiddy. (Don't witch with thet draft
ter thet stove, 'Mandy; you'll git it out o' kilter,
fuzzino.) Black daisy tea 's real good f'r them
distressed spells like she hes; it's both liv'nin'
and stringth'nin', ez ole Aunt Rooty uster say.
Well, an' howsumever come you deown here
ter-day, Mis' Crandall, clear way deown from
the 'ville? "

"Well, the way on 't was, their father, he took
a notion to a pair o' steers somewhere's down on

Pine Judy Pint, an' he's gonter study on 'em awhile, an' lef' me here ter do some tradin'. Well, I expect I hed oughter be tendin' toc it."

"Well, good-day, Mis' Crandall. I dono's I shall ever git up thet far to where you live. I don't git no time f'r visitin' 'n' sech."

"I'm afeerd, Mis' Tift, you'm too smart ter gin yerself no chance, but you oughter take a time 'n' come 'n' see us."

"Well, ef I be any smarter than the next one its force put, thet's all. My will's good ter be lazy, jest the same's ary one on 'em. Lor', I sh'd like ter lay abed ev'ry mawnin o' my life tell five o'clock, ef so be 't I could. But I sh'll come up, ef I ken 's well 's not."

"So do. An' ef ever I go pahst y'r house I sh'll 'light 'n' see your folks."

"We shell be very pleased ter see ye, any time," rather curtly replied the business-like Mis' Tift, closing the interchange of compliments, and resuming her bargaining, which she soon completed with signal success.

"Ma, ma," bleated the eager 'Mandy, holding her mother by her gown, "don't go yit. Say, git me a new frock off'n this here piece o' pink muslin-de-laine. Oh, I do want a boughten frock so dretful bad!"

"Yes, you'd like ter be reeled in silk, would n't ye?" returned the severe parent. "Now, don't you w'ine, 'Mandy. I wish't my head would n't ache tell I git ye sech a frock; so you study on thet a while."

Headaches were all but unknown to the matron, save in the uses of rhetoric, but 'Mandy was sufficiently experienced in the significance of the phrase just launched at her to resign herself to the inevitable, as she and her mother departed, soon followed by Mis' Crandall.

The sole comment made in the conclave of loungers upon this meeting was the indiscreet utterance of the adolescent Sol Simms to Hi Collins, an equally simple youth.

" Ain't it queer, though," remarked the observant Sol, " heow Mis' Teft never will let on ez she's well 's common, when all the time she dooz look stout 'n' rugged 'nough, 'cordin' ter my notion, t' eat puddin' 'ith a barnshovel!"

This attempt at wit was coldly received, Mis' Tift being the wife of a man of considerable rustic importance; and Sol made no further effort to shine in the conversation until his return after doing the afternoon chores, to join the group that gathered around the cylinder stove, in which crackled a hospitable fire of " lightwood," and which was raised above a shallow box filled with sawdust, and much in need of a fresh supply of the same. Jim Fones had made the usual sly preparation for his evening guests by setting the clock ahead, and, as custom required, they would govern themselves in accordance with the simple device.

The bucolic types of which this informal club was composed were, with few exceptions, such as to develop in the observer a vigorous revolt from the binding force of the Miltonic example of homage to the human face divine. Looking upon some of these heavy countenances, with nothing of adolescence but its crudeness of contour, or nothing of age but its lined and seamed ugliness, one was fain to read backward the meaning of that inexpressibly moving cry of longing after visible human companionship uttered from the solitudes of rayless darkness, and to declare that the poet was blind indeed to the physical faults of Adam's lineage, known to him in all its imperfections until exalted by the idealizing touch born of a hopeless desire.

For instance, there was Sol Simms. This adolescent was the exact similitude of a gander. Every ludicrous point of resemblance was there, — the long craning neck, the insignificant, close-cropped, whitish head, the round, reddened eyes, the protruding beak, the abruptly retreating chin, — all these marking him, no less than his long flapping arms, strident voice, and uncouth gait, as being at no distant remove from those clothed figures of animals which usually pass for caricatures, but which might occasionally be esteemed genuine likenesses.

In effective antithesis to this specimen of ungainly youth was the spectacle of fine old age afforded by Uncle Josey Austin, a handsome old man, with clear-cut features and flowing white hair and beard. As sometimes happens in such cases, Nature had forgotten to put as large a supply of brains behind that picturesque mask as the fitness of things might seem to require, and hence, perhaps, the familiarity with which he was still addressed by his nickname, and the freedom with which children claimed his society.

"Why, whiar's my stick gone to?" mildly inquired Uncle Josey, soon after taking his seat. " I brung't in, sure-ly."

" Thiar 't is, Uncle, over thiar, right behind ye," chorused the company.

"Ef 't hed ben a b'ar, 't would a bitten ye," observed Jim Fones, and the ready rustic laugh went round at the time-honored bit of pleasantry.

" Say, Uncle Josey, Uncle Josey, tell us the b'ar story," clamored the children of the house, who were still hovering about the store, in imminent peril of being sent to bed.

" Oh, neow, childring," returned the old man, in his plaintive drawling intonation, "ye don't wanter hear Jimmy's story fust-off, do ye? Don't Sukey, a little dear, wanter hear her story, all abeout the harp that scounded seven miles above greound, 'n' seven miles under greound, 'n' seven miles beyond sea?"

"No," stoutly insisted the dominant Jimmy,
"me 'n' Sukey wants ter hear 'bout the b'ars."

"Wal, then," replied their aged friend,
"Jimmy mus' come 'n' set right here, next ter
me, 'n' Sukey 'll come up on the old man's knee
— oops-a-daisy! here she be! Wal, onct upon
a time, the' was a little boy 't lived all alone with
his mother, 'n' one day he took his bahsket 'n'
went out inter the woods ter pick huckleberries.
Wal, he went, 'n' he went, 'n' he went along a
leetle furder, 'n' he come toe a grahssy place, 'n'
then he come toe a middlin' rocky place, 'n'
bimeby he diskivered a b'ar's den, with three
little b'ars, all cuggled down in it. Wal, he
tucked up them little b'ars in his bahsket, all
nice, 'n' he buckled f'r home. So he went
along, an' along, an' along, an' he was jest a sayin' to hisself how dretful pleased his mother 'd be
ter see them little b'ars, when all toe onct he
heered suthin' behind him, going brookety,
brookety, brook, an' he turned an' he looked,
an' he see the old she b'ar comin' right arter
him."

Here Uncle Josey paused to give place to
the *ows* and *owtches* of his hearers, who were
quivering in the fearful joy awakened by the
narrative.

"Wal," pursued the story-teller, "the little
boy he run, but 't wa'n't no kinder use; the ole
b'ar was gittin' clus' up with him, when he jes'

throwed out one o' the little b'ars, 'thout stoppin'
ter look behind him. Wal, the ole b'ar she nosed
him, 'n' licked him, 'n' picked him up, 'n' carr'd
him off, 'n' laid him down in the den."

The same history was related concerning the
second cub, after which recital, —

" So now the little boy was mos' outer the
woods, when jes' ez he come in sight o' home
an' he could see the clo'es hangin' out on the
line, all of a suddint he heerd suthin' behind him
goin' brookety, brookety, brookety, *brook*, an'
there she was codgwallopin' along arter him ; an'
he pitched out the larst little b'ar 'n' run lickety
cut, lickety cut, 'n' he got saft home. And his
mother was overjoyed ter see him."

The children disappeared soon after the close
of their favorite tale, but the youths of the
neighborhood, seated beside the counter, which
was lighted ·by the whale-oil lamp and the
tallow candle, were pursuing the evening amusement of playing fox and geese with grains of
corn, and of puzzling out, with the help of slate
and pencil, the traditionary rebus, " I understand that you under-take toe over-throw my
under-takings."

In the circle around the stove the enlivening
influences of snuff and tobacco kept the sources
of conversational flow fully supplied. The usual
comments upon the weather and the crops were
duly exchanged. Uncle Josey predicted a "con-

sid'ble warm spell, on the stringth o' the almanac," though, as he added with mild scepticism, it did n't always tell right.   Uncle Cy
Card, the carpenter, related some instructive
reminiscences of a December famous in local
annals, when he and the rest o' the gang worked
at a raisin' in their shirt-sleeves; but it was the
general sense of the company that winter never
rots in the skies.   Old Polypus Pollock, a prey
to the eccentricity of the paternal taste in nomenclature, and an inheritor of an inordinate
love of mysterious phrases, related with exhaustive minuteness the history of his successful
potato crop.

" Yes," he complacently observed, " I do
b'leeve I raised them 'ere p'taters ez a crop hed
oughter be raised.   I 'clar' for 't, I did n't gin
'em no peace.   I jest hoed an' weeded, an'
weeded an' hoed, all summer; the' wa'n't no let
up to 't; an' them p'taters did grow sponta-
nously, toe be sure," he concluded, with a
thoughtful air.

" What be ye goin' ter git f'r 'em, Pol? " was
the sharp inquiry of the astute Pindar Pryor.

" Wal, I ain't figgered it eout so fearful clus',
yit.   Ez *you* say, neighbor" (with urbanity) " they
be terr'ble big.   But I don't hold to none of
these here 'nonymous high prices; a good, fa'r,
promis'cous price is all 't *I* calc'late on."

" Taters ain't what they uster be," mildly

complained Uncle Josey; "they don't taste *'tatery* this fall."

"Of all the poor livin' 't ever I don't wanter see," dryly observed a dyspeptic-looking man, who had not passed unscathed through the ordeal of "boarding around" when in his early years he had done the State some service as a schoolmaster, but without sacrificing native dialect to artificial book-learning, "'t was jest about the most mis'able down to Number Twenty-five, when I taught school there. Cipherin' all day with the boys, an livin' on them mean johnnycakes made 'thout a drop o' milk, was ruther too tough f'r me." He paid the tribute of a longdrawn yawn to the melancholy recollection.

The staple topics being well-nigh disposed of, a silence fell, dedicated to the influences of the soothing weed, until all were suddenly aroused into welcome activity by the arrival of a neighbor who, coming post-haste from a house of sickness, briefly announced the animating intelligence —

"Wal, Pardon Sherman's dead, — died this arternoon, at twelve minutes past six o'clock."

"I wanter know, now," was the refreshing expletive in which Uncle Cy indulged; "Left no much prop'ty, I guess," was the characteristic note sharply sounded by the keen-visaged Pindar Pryor; and "Wal, wal, he were a very likely man," was Uncle Josey's ready word of

obituary eulogy, uttered with sundry edifying
head-shakings, and lugubrious "sithes," as he
would have named them.

"Ez toe thet ar," portentously announced
Steve Reynolds, or "Runnuls," a rough, middle-
aged man, not devoid of a certain air of homely
wash-and-wear wisdom, " I ain't so sure who is
likely, and who ain't. I don't mean no affront
to nobody nor no disrespec' ter the dead, but
sech news as this here dooz allers call ter mind
thet ar' 't we uster read ter school in the 'C'lum-
bian Orator,' when one o' them old wiseacres
says, says he, 'Call no man happy till the eend
on his days,' or some sech a saw ez thet.
Now, I ain't no flosopher," modestly continued
Steve, " but I sh'd go a leetle furder 'n thet, 'n'
I sh'd say, Don't go ter callin' no man good tell
he's ben buried a year an' a half, an' the grahss
hes growed up over him. F'r I 've noticed in
my time," pursued Steve, fixedly regarding his
audience while slowly shifting his quid, "thet
with thet there graveyard grahss the 's apt to
spring up another crop thet ain't so handy. I
tell 'em, the Scriptur says, 'Death 's the Prince o'
Darkness,' but the' is times when he brings a lot
of ugly things ter light. What 's thet you 'm a
blurtin' out there, Sol Simms?"

"Why, sa-ay," stammered Sol, with phenom-
enal smartness on being thus encouraged,
"there's old Aunt Patty, up 't ourus" (he

referred to his great-aunt, a member of the
household), " she's so good 't she's bad. It's
dretful mithersome ter hev her 'round sometimes, 'f'r when anybody else 'd be mad ez a hoe,
she won't lay no blame ter nobody. But I ground
her grist f'r her yist'd'y. Says I, speakin' up
loud's I could, pretty nigh, f'r the old lady's
deef's an adder, ' Aunt Patty, you 'm so mortle
charit'ble 't you allers says about folks under
sixty, ef they 'm cross or wrong-behaved, thet
they 'm sick an' can't help theirselves, an' ef
they 'm over sixty, why then they 'm childish
an' dono no better; ' an' she laffed an' said,
' Git along, y'r father uster tell me so long afore
you was born.' "

The more practical members of the conference had ill-brooked the delay imposed by these
unprofitable moralizings, and now obtained from
the willing narrator full particulars of the lamented event. Curiosity being allayed, specu-
lation next ran rife.

" S'pose the widder 'n the gals c'n jest about
make out ter ruggle along, cain't they? " queried
Uncle Cy, with a furrowed brow, while his neglected pipe nearly went out, in his spasm of
neighborly anxiety.

" Mebbe some on 'em 'll git marr'd," was the
brilliant suggestion of Jim Fones.

" I dono, I *dono*," pondered Uncle Josey,
with profound sympathy; " they ain't none on

'em very fanciful, an' Almiry's got a reg'lar
drive-on-carter look to her."

"*What* sorter look?" questioned Sol Simms,
with interest.

"Don't you know thet story, sonny? Wal,
away back in some o' them old times, the' was
a man gonter be hung, 'n' they said how they'd
gin him a pardon ef so be 't he could git anybody ter hev him, 'n' a woman 't come along said
she would. So he riz up in the cart ter see her,
an' when he see her he lay down agin. 'Long
nose, an' crooked chin,' says he; 'drive on,
carter.'"

"Looker here, Mr. Runnuls," broke in Hi
Collins, addressing Steve, "the 's a gal livin' out,
down to the bridge, thet come from up north,
som'ers to the northern fac'tries, an' she 's the
most ig'nant kind. She never see chicken an'
quohaug pie, an' she did n't know what con-
queedles was!"

"Quonqueedles, gran'futher calls 'em," remarked Steve. "Quonqueedles was the name
the old Injuns giv' 'em, 'cordin' ter his tell. I
sh'd reckon it come from their n'ise, when
they'm a sorter tunin' up. The' was a man
come here from some o' them northern parts,
called 'em bob-o-links. I expect thet ar' out-
landlish name come right down from some o'
them dangerous old Massachusetts Prisbyter'ans.
Uster go spyin' 'round arter upland liverwort,

an' called 'em Mayflowers, I b'lieve. He was a
gret han' f'r sech truck.

"I dono 's you reck'lect," joined in Uncle
Josey, "thet furrin' sort o' creeter, from York
or Pensylvany, I b'lieve."

"What, old Christian Tim's raskill son-in-
law?" asked Steve. "How the ole man uster
go on 'bout him! Says he, 'His name was
Awle, an' he tho't he *was* all, an' he *took* all,
an' he *hed* all.'"

"Jes' so. Wal, he uster tell it f'r true thet
whar he come from the women-folks allers
milked the ceows."

"Sho!" exclaimed 'Lias Simins, an hitherto
silent little man, now wearing the air of having
been forcibly struck in the face by a missile
from that boomerang which Dr. Holmes says
is the weapon carried by the man of facts in a
social company; then, with a rapid adjustment
of his quickened intellects to the new situation,
"Wal, I vow, they hed oughter!" he announced,
with an explosive energy that provoked a loud
laugh, — it being the general understanding that
Dame Simins was one who knew her rights,
and, knowing, dared maintain.

"I ain't much knowin' ter furriners," cau-
tiously preluded the cross-roads blacksmith, Jenk-
son Castle, "don't know, — cain't tell — hain't
seen, — but I've hearn tell 't they'm hed three
on 'em up 't the big house this summer stid o'

squaws." (African squaws were in his mind.)
" Three I-rish maids," they *said*, he repeated,
carefully, as one speaking under possible cor-
rection. " I never see 'em myself, I say, but
my woman, she's ben up there with huckleberries, an' she spoke well on 'em too. Said
they treated on her harnsome, very harnsome.
an' gin' her a dish o' tea. But it stan's to reason they cain't airn the salt ter their porridge
up there. Nothin' ter do, ez ye may say, but
set 'n' suck their paws, like a woodchuck in
Jenooary."

" 'T was an I-rish fellar laid thet new piece o'
stun wall out ter the Dilly Carly place, ter the
old mill," observed Steve. " Ky-arn Driscoll,
his name was."

" What, toe the old Twin Chimbley house?"
queried the blacksmith, with a quickened accent.
" I wanter know! Wal, I would n't tho't one on
'em could airn fo'pence-ha'penny a day. I
calc'lated they was jest fit ter cooter 'round.
But Nailer Tom told me thet was a harnsome
piece o' work. He never said who done it,
though."

From these practical topics a transition was
gradually made, as the evening wore on, to
those of a less definite character; and with
the return to weather-speculations came a discussion as to that weather-breeder, the Pala-
tine Light. Steve's great yellow cur yawned

cavernously, as if he thought it a stale and
unprofitable subject, but his master paid due
attention to the spokesman of the moment.

"I hayve saw," said Uncle Josey, speaking
with the modest confidence of one who knew
how, on occasion, to keep his footing among
the treacherous parts of speech. "I hayve saw
them ez seed the ole Pal'tine with their own
livin', breathin' eyes."

"Why, the Jedge see it, time an' agin, on
the ole Queen's Anne road, did n't he?" trucu-
lently demanded, with an air as of personal
resentment, Zach Humford, a kind of human
grasshopper in voice and "build."

"No," demurred Steve, guardedly, "I dono's
he ever said 's he see it over 'n above onct or
twicet."

"Wal," fiercely returned the grasshopper, who
gave every indication of becoming a burden,
"this I will say, an' stan' to it, the Jedge were
a very likely man."

"Nothin' agin' thet, neighbor," spoke Steve,
concisely, but heartily.

"He *were* a likely man, I say," retorted the
grasshopper, with the air of having been flatly
contradicted, "a ve-ry likely man"—swinging
a heavily booted leg, and viciously kicking the
wood-box—"and I don't keer a fiddle-string
who hears me say it."

"S'pos'in we sh'd ax Gran'futher Runnuls

about it," suggested the pacific Uncle Josey.
"I sh'd railly like ter hear the ole gentleman
talk," he added, with the patronizing tolerance
of age for senility.

"Gran'futher Runnuls," who held that rela-
tion to the middle-aged Steve, had thus far
remained a dormant intelligence, isolated by
his deafness, but tranquilly absorbing the warmth
of the fire into his lean, old-world figure. His
long white hair was tied in a black ribbon
queue, but a gay bandanna handkerchief pro-
tected his crown. His eyes still twinkled keenly
beneath his frosty brows.

"Better not git gran'futher started," warned
Steve. "He ain't so easy to wind up, when ye
git through with him, now I tell ye. He's an
old, aged man, gran'futher is."

"I'll resk him," snapped the grasshopper,
spurred on by this opposition to put himself in
communication with the patriarch by shouting
in his ear.

"Say, Gran'futher, tell us all about the
Pal'tine, 'n' who see it, won't ye?"

"Yes, yes," responded the ancient one, apparently in cheerful assent, "Yes, I'm a gret age,
I am. Nigh upon ninety year old, most ninety
odd. I'm the oldes' freeman in this here town,
sir!"

"Stop, he hearn ye well 'nough," spoke Steve,
arresting the grasshopper in another attempt at

dictation. "He hears ye, but he won't hear *too* ye. He allers goes on thet way awhile." (Steve had a manner as of calling attention to some curious, but slightly damaged piece of mechanism.) "Lor', he don't sc'ace ever notice what you say, but goes 'n' tells over a lurry all 'bout his age, jest like some youngster 't says, 'I'm half-past ten, goin' on 'leven.' He's proud ez a peacock on his age, an' now you'm spoke to him, bimeby he'll tell ye somethin', but he don't take no orders from folks. Seems so he's way off, kinder, 'n' you couldn't git at him, noway." Steve sawed the air vaguely but vigorously with both arms, in the endeavor to express these metaphysical niceties. "There, he's most ready," he continued, and gestured, as if he had said of a venerable time-piece, "Hark, she's a-goin' ter strike!"

"Neighbors an' frien's," began the patriarch, lifting his head, and speaking in a quaint tone of old-time mannerliness. "I ben a thinkin', while settin' here, ez the Quakers says [this seemed to be some antiquated relic of pleasantry] abeout them times inter the old Rev'lution."

"My glory!" loudly exclaimed Sol Simms to his crony, Hi Collins, "be thet old critter a steerin' full tilt f'r them red-coats agin?"

"I ain't heerd him meander on about 'em mor' 'n forty-'leven times, hev you, Sol?" returned the brilliant Collins, with fine sarcastic power.

"Le's go 'long!" suggested Sol; which they
did, with much clumping of awkward feet in
clumsy boots.

Of those who remained it might be said that

> "They all sat round in attitudes
> Of various dejection,"

as, with a bright and happy look, the aged narrator began, after a rather rambling fashion, —

· "Many's the time our folks hes talked it over,
how the red-coats come here. I wa'n't to home
then, ye know. I was up to Exeter, livin' eout
with some o' the quality. Most all on the Tory
folks went 'n' staid up there them times. Wal,
't was to No'thup's the red-coats brung up fust.
The folks heerd a n'ise in the dead o' night, 'n'
when they looked out, the yard was full o' red-
coats. Them was cur'ous times. They fired a
bullet through the front door, jes' ter let 'em
know they was comin' in, I s'pose. The bullet
hole's there ter this day, ye know. No'thup's
folks never would hev' it teched.

"Wal, No'thup's three ahnts was a livin' with
him, toe the old place. Them No'thup gals was
kinder gittin' along. They was mighty nigh of
an age, but Tabithy, she was the youngest on
'em, why, she must ha' ben nigh upon eighty
year old. She slep' alone in the sto' bedroom,
'n' when she heerd the n'ise 'n' commotion in the
house, 'n' the trampin' o' the red-coats, she riz
up in bed, jest ez the hull posse on 'em got ter

her door, 'n' was filin' in. She sot up 'mazin
stiff, f'r she'd allers slep' in her stays, an' her
nightkip nodded kind of awful, an' says she,
pretty middlin' starn, but her v'ice sort o' dyin'
away into an eecho, toe the larst on it, 'What
be you folks a-doin' on?' The head man on
'em, says he, quick enough, 'Quiet y'rself,
marm, we'm on'y a sarchin' f'r men.' But with
thet she giv' a screech — a tol'able loud one —
'Wha-a-t! Sarchin' f'r men, in *my* room!' an'
flinged herself back on the piller, in conniption
fits, an' swoonded dead away. Wal, I s'pose
she felt obleeged to," pondered the narrator,
considerately. "But she hed ter come *to* herself *by* herself, f'r the' wa'n't nobody ter pay no
'tention to her; the red-coats was in airnest, an'
they kep' a sarchin' an' a sarchin' in ev'ry hole
an' corner, tell they lighted on Mr. No'thup, ez
he was purtectin' his prop'ty from a p'sition
he'd took up under the gret heap o' wool under
the eaves in the garr't. Wal, they took him an'
yoked him up, and carr'd him off ter Newport f'r
a dan-ger-ous rebel. But the best on't was
when they was on the way, a-marchin' past the
old Squire's, where toe thet self-same time the'
was a comp'ny of Cont'nentals a quartered in
the gret room, — eighty on 'em slep' all over the
floor. One on 'em had seen some sarvice, —
I've hearn tell he'd shot a dead Hessian; but
howsumever, thet's neither here nor there.

Wal, the head man o' them red-coats, — the cen-
tur*i*on, I sh'd call him, — he come all to a halt,
an' says he ter No'thup, 'What's the politics
with these here?' Mr. No'thup, says he, 'Oh,
they'm all peaceable folks, very peaceable.'
'Humph,' says he agin, wheelin' round on him
kinder short, 'What's the meanin' o' all them
there lights?' An' them was the watch-lights
the sogers burnt, but never knowed a breath
about who an' what was near 'em. 'Wal,' says
No'thup, 'they'm got a child thet's terr'ble apt
ter hev the croup, an' 't ain't no oncommon sight
ter see lights 'roun' there any time o' night.'
So fin'lly he was pacified, an' they moved on;
but the old Squire never hed chick nor child
in his life, an' how he happened to think on't,
No'thup uster say, he never did rightly know.
It was clear luck an' chance f'r 'em. He knowed
that ar' custguard, ez they called 'em, wa'n't
very fit ter wrastle with reg'lars. Most they was
good for, the Squire's wife tho't, was ter keep
bread from mouldin'. She wa'n't very frien'ly
to 'em, an' they writ up all 'roun' the walls o'
the gret room, 'Hang the old she-Tory!' The
Squire was ev'ry bit an' grain's much a Tory ez
she was, but he did n't say nothin', ye see. She
would sputter right out, 'n' thet's how she got
the Squire inter trouble, so 't the Committee o'
Safety kep' an eye on him, an' quartered them
troops on him. Wal, she was high-sperited, an'

8

things was gettin' middlin' bitter, but it run along, an' so, fin'lly — "

" Look here, gran'futher!" interrupted Steve, manfully stemming the swelling tide of reminiscence, "time to be goin', now!"

" Don't you go to discumboberate me, Steve," complained the aged one, after a pause, and a slight start. " I b'lieve I was jest goin' ter say suthin'."

" Wal, say it ter home, then," roughly but not unkindly returned tho grandson, tendering his sire his walking-stick. " They'm most all gone home now. Nine o'clock! Jim's a shuttin' up! Say, Jim, fasten up tight ter keep out them red-coats ter night, ye know," he jocosely admonished, as, closing the door behind him, he adjusted his sturdy tread to the shuffling steps of age, and the two groped homeward in the darkness, while the whip-poor-will's wild note sounded again and yet again from the wooded hill that overhung their pathway. ·

EARLY planting time had begun with the softly-overcast April days, and Uncle 'Sias Grumly's fields were rich with the moist warm browns of the freshly turned furrows, traced by the toil of Stout and Starling, the ungainly oxen that now stood with bowed heads, rigid as monoliths, while waiting to be unyoked by their master and his hired man, Brandywine Spears.

The west was bright with that peculiarly vivid yellow light that is usually a precursor of rain. Touched by this transitory radiance, which streamed richly from beneath an overhanging mass of densely purpling vapors, the stretches of bushy pasture, and the wooded uplands, glittering with moisture and aglow with the almost autumnal brilliancy of early leafage, were quickened into a burst of magical bloom and brightness. The unearthly splendor was repeated in the shining links and windings of the sinuous Quacataug Pond, which, by Nature's massive mimicry, simulated a river of many turns, with sudden surprises of narrowing channels and devices of semi-islands that became peninsulas at

low water. The same law of caprice and change
reappeared in the diversity of its banks, which
afforded the alternate varieties of grassy slopes
and wooded, rocky steeps. Young white birches
of an airy, feminine grace, stood bathing their
feet in the ripples, like veritable dryads, or
danced to the light breeze that sprang up at
sunset, quickening the mobile play of the sensitive waters; and aged, dying white birches,
caught fast in the myriad tangles of the drooping gray moss, piteously lifted their fettered and
withered limbs, like victims wreathed for druid-
ical sacrifice. A group of blighted sycamores
on a hill overlooking the lake, the leopardine
markings of their trunks relieved against the
blackening sky, began to wave their tortured
branches with a warning murmur, breathing of
night and storm. The soldier blackbirds, though
displaying their gay red wings with all their
customary twilight flutter and bustle, yet seemed
to tune their closing bugle-song with an occasional note of serious preparation for hostile
weather.

But the warm yellow light in the west still lin-
gered, bathing the whole stretch of country in a
transfiguring glow which held the eye with almost the same effect of a sudden revelation of
new beauty in familiar scenes as is afforded by
the magical touches of a light snowfall; though
the darkening clouds constantly lowered upon

the horizon, fast obscuring the parting smile of
the many-minded April day.

"Open an' shet, sign o' wet," sapiently commented Brandywine Spears, who, while awaiting
the call to supper, was whittling at a small block
intended as a wheel for the toy go-cart which he
was rudely fashioning for his youthful son.

"'T won't hender 'em none," replied Uncle
'Sias, from his momentary resting-place on the
horse-block, and speaking with a certain asper-
ity of tone, evidently addressed to some latent
quality of his companion's manner and intent.
"These here young converts ain't none of y'r
fair-weather Christians."

"No, *thet* they ain't," emphatically admitted
the other, with the suspicious facility of an opin-
ionated opponent who has a telling point to
make; "it's the fair weather, yer know, thet's
goin' ter be too much f'r 'em, putty soon, Uncle
'Sias. An airly spring, ez it mought be this
here, an' sultry days comin' on so fast is turrible
tryin' ter young converts. Th' ole Elder — I
heerd him exhortin' of 'em las' Thu'sd'y evenin',
down ter the schoolus meetin' — .

"Beware, Brandywine," interrupted honest
Uncle 'Sias, with genuine concern, " lest, havin'
enj'yed the means o' grace, yer should y'rself be
a castaway."

"Wal, ez I was a-sayin'," pursued the undis-
mayed serving-man, acknowledging this warning

only by a dry nod, " he gin 'em consid'ble of a
talkin' to.   Told 'em how they was the bloomin'
harvest of a precious revival season.   Plants o'
grace, he called 'em.   Wal, mebbe they be ; but
they 'm   mighty   short-lived ones.   Yer know
well 'nough how 't is with the heft on 'em, Uncle
'Sias.   Takes all winter long, in the fust place,
ter git 'em started.   Paul plantin' an' 'Pollos
waterin', an' all the women-folks, in a go-round
continooally on account of 'em.   'Long about
March, they do 'pear ter take holt some, an' all
toe onct, clear away they go, heightin' up in a
gret growth, ekil ter Jonah's gourd.   'Bout the
latter eend o' Aprile, some on 'em gits kinder
spindlin'.   They can't stand warm weather, noway
in the world ; the May sun wilts 'em clean down
ter the ground ; an' time June comes in, what
with fishin', an' layin' round in the shade, an'
goin' down the pond, an' — an' sich — they 'm
all broke up f'r meetin' folks.   All flesh is grahss,
I expect, Uncle 'Sias, saints 'n' sinners 'n' all."

" Ef yer would n't go down the pond so much
yerself, Brandywine Spears, 'long of a jug with
a corn-cob stopple, an' I won't say jest what in-
side on it," admonished Uncle 'Sias, with wholesome severity, " mebbe yer wouldn't fault the
Lord's work an' the Lord's sarvants so much."

" Wal, Uncle, mebbe you 'm got the right
on 't there," confessed the unabashed culprit,
with calmly philosophic equipoise, " an' mebbe

I'm in the right on 't in my notions consarnin'
these here young folks," he continued, with persistent scepticism. " Ef our foresight was as
good as our hindsight, we sh'd all on us done
diff'rent by times, *I* expect; but them new
converts — shucks ! Uncle 'Sias, you an' me's
seen a long lot on 'em, an' *I* never see the time
yit when the month o' May wa'n't a mighty
criticle junctur f'r 'em."

The call to supper filled the pause that Uncle
'Sias apparently deemed it fruitless to occupy
with further admonitions; and pious yeoman
and sceptical swain were presently sharing the
bounties of the board, around which the household had first stood, while the former with closed
eyes repeated, in slightly Puritanic accents, a
long-drawn grace.

Aunt Freelove Grumly, Uncle 'Sias's wife, presided at the supper, having previously completed
her toilet for the evening exercises by donning
even such superfluities of dress as shoes and
stockings. Great-aunt Grumly, a frugal eater,
who never took supper, sat rigidly upright on
the dye-tub in the chimney corner, vigorously
knitting, her long apron-strings tied round her
waist to keep steady a corn cob that formed her
knitting-sheath. A box of the ever useful cobs,
spared from those that were stored for the process of curing the hams and the " buckies " of
last season, stood ready to be carried to the

Franklin stove in the damp and musty " great room," where the meeting would be held.   The grandchildren of the house were building log-cabins from the abundant store, the girl intent on her toppling cobhouse, and the boy just deserting his structure to deck himself with a pasteboard helmet, edged with a circlet of turkey feathers, the better to " play Injun " by rushing with ruthless uproar upon a rather phlegmatic baby, creeping in tortoise-like attitudes on the fireplace-hearth, and bearing marks of having painfully traversed the sandy desert that occu-pied the centre of the room, and which with careful strokes of the broom, had been adorned with the approved " herring-bone " pattern.

"Deary me, Nate," mildly expostulated his grandmother, "you'll skeer the baby out of a year's growth.   There, you'm fairly skeered the wits out of him," she continued, as the infant, transfixed between wonder and terror, decided for the latter emotion, and gave it voice, with gratifying evidence of lung-power.

"Guess not," tartly remarked Great-aunt Grumly, who favored the sprightly Nate, and failed to see in the babe a child of promise. "I'll resk him.   Nought's never in danger, ez ever I heerd tell on ! "

. The rain, which had fallen in occasional warm " fog-showers " through the day, but had held up, as Uncle 'Sias said, for a milkin' slatch, had

not yet begun again, and the attendants upon
the series of house-to-house meetings that were
holden as the sequelæ of the recent revival,
began to arrive in numbers that implied as full
possession of the premises as if the summons
had been a funereal one.   Not only the great
room, where the Elder sat, behind the light-
stand and Bible, with the high mantelpiece,
ranged with home-made candles, for a background, was occupied; but the borrowed chairs
of the occasion scraped and creaked on the
floors, painted and unpainted, floors sanded or
scantily rug-covered, of the lower story.   Parlor,
kitchen, and bedroom adjoining the two were
fast filling with a company presumably including
that personage so often affectionately inquired
for by Elder Bayles, in his favorite form of
appeal opening with the rhetorical supposition,
"If there's a sinner here to-night, within the
sound of my voice," — a use of the subjunctive
mood which did but scant justice to the searching qualities of that powerful and piercing
organ.   The "Elder's" official claims to bear
that Scriptural designation were not, perhaps,
very clearly made out; but he was rated as a
highly acceptable leader of the domestic meetings; and none of his hearers were prone to
give themselves any anxiety about the exact
spiritual value of his brevet title, so long as they
found his manner a satisfactory compromise

between that of the minister 'and the layman, and continued to esteem him a much "smarter" speaker than others of more assured ecclesiastical position, — as, for instance, the wandering Elder Nahum Holley, who, on this occasion, was simply tolerated as a second in the leadership of the evening's devotion.

These devotions were, like those of more sophisticated people, things of mixed motive and various results. The unknown writer of some popular rhymes, which succinctly relate the different causes promoting the assembling at. church of a congregation in town, and ending with this characterization of a faithful few, "And some go there to worship God," would have found equal scope for his satire in the rustic prayer-meeting. So long as the mingling qualities of human nature remain an indivisible compound of fine gold and coarse clay, so long will the satirist and the humorist find a legitimate field of observation in every popular gathing, whether met for mirth or mourning, for local government or social worship. Neither we nor our neighbors can divest ourselves of our human attributes, even in our prayers and hymns; and the smile with which we note the incidental humors of the hour does no wrong to the respect with which we regard its serious motives. Nay, it may be as harmless as even the earnestness of the simple souls to whom

certain observances that are perhaps things
remote from our needs bring a genuine spiritual
refreshment.   To the worthy Uncle 'Sias and
his peers, welcoming as they did the influences
of the special form of religious sentiment in
which they had been reared, there was no dero-
gation from the honor due to sacred offices in
thus administering them without obvious cause
beneath a roof associated only with the common
uses of life.   " The beauty of holiness," as man-
ifested in the outward decencies of worship, was
a meaningless phrase to him and his spiritual
kin.   Let it be granted that they might be none
the worse, in the tougher texture of their moral
fabric, for this deprivation; yet it is certain that
they were none the more fortunate, in the last
development of their higher qualities, for the
conditions to which they were born.   Says an
able student of the history of our progressive
civilization: " It has come to pass, from a
variety of causes, that religion is offered to the
eyes of this nation, for the most part, under a
contemptible aspect, and without those accesso-
ries which strike the senses and move the heart
with a due apprehension of her heavenly origin,
and of a dignity and greatness above the common way of the world."   The same observer
would further have said of such surroundings of
this scene as the high-piled feather bed of state
in the corner of the great room, the litter of cobs

around the stove, and Aunt Freelove's best
bonnet and shawl grotesquely occupying the
settee, " These are accompaniments of a secular-
izing of religion, whereby she is stripped of the
reverence which is her own, and exposed to an
unjust humiliation."

These untoward influences, inseparable from
the presence of the familiar surroundings, might
possibly be traced in the riotous demeanor of
Uncle 'Sias's twin grandsons, Nate and Date,
over whom he daily lamented as " the most mis-
chievousest wild colts 't ever he see" and who
could only be withheld by the sternest watching,
and by whispered threats (made with a curiously
unconscious disparagement of the nature of religious privileges) of holding a season of prayer
over them when the folks were gone, from indulging in unseemly demonstrations of humorous delight in Elder Holley's well-known peculiarities
of twitching his shaggy eyebrows, rolling his grotesquely heavy head, and displaying other John-
sonian contortions of countenance, — thus mani-
festing his sympathy with the devotion of the
presiding elder in his opening prayer.   Great-
aunt Grumly, always a rather "fractious" old
lady, and no easy subject of admonition, set an
indecorous example by persisting in her knitting;
and when Uncle 'Sias, regardless of his painfully
audible " squeak-leather" boots, made his slow
way up to her with a whispered remonstrance,

she testily responded, with a peevish clicking of her needles, and by no means in smothered tones : —

" Lemme 'lone, 'Sias, lemme 'lone; 't won't hender Sim Bayles's prayin' none ef I do reel off a bout or two on y'r socks. Lord knows ye hain't got a hull pair ter yer feet, now."

Some of the young people who were grouped in conveniently retired corners were severely overtaken with giggles at this frank announcement, and suffered comical agonies; or, as they expressed it afterwards, they thought die they should. Uncle 'Sias looked worried and anxious. It really seemed as if the Puritan tithing-man, with his rod of office for the discipline of such offenders, were an indispensable functionary of the farmhouse prayer-meeting. Few other interruptions followed just then, however, except that a young woman who had insisted on coming to the meeting while undergoing an attack of toothache, whose swollen features were bandaged with a folded handkerchief pinned beneath the chin, and who from time to time leaned her head wearily in her mother's lap, naturally felt privileged to utter an occasional groan; which might be interpreted to edification, as signifying concern of mind no less than distress of body. Also, an aged sister, commonly called, without regard to her proper name, Aunt Rooty, from her vocation as a purveyor of simples, being

afflicted with stoutness and deafness, and occupying one of the chief seats, was armed with a
huge, rustling palm-leaf fan, and flagellated
herself therewith, in an aggressively noisy
fashion, inaudible to herself, but which might
have grated harshly upon the nerves of sensitive listeners.

The prayer went on, nevertheless, to the satisfaction of the hearers, to whom it was frankly
addressed, under the very thin veil of an occasional form of supplication. Nobody's gravity
was moved when, by a slight confusion of ideas,
the speaker, in remembering a bereaved family
of the neighborhood, prayed fervently for the
parents of the poor little orphan that lay in the
coffin; nobody found it noticeable when he
corrected a trifling misstatement which he had
inadvertently made, and amended his petition
in behalf of "an afflicted brother of this town,"
by catching himself up with the words, "or, I
would say, jest over the line, inter Exeter, but"
(on further reflection, and in an off-hand tone)
" O Lord, it ain't partickerler which; " nobody
in the assemblage was startled when in closing
he prayed with superfluous fervor that iniquity
might be showered down plenteously upon all
of them; for such as these were his staple
phrases, of which any one of his audience
might have said, in Dr. Holland's words: —

" And I suppose, that in his prayers and

graces, I've heard them all at least a thousand times."

An unacceptable brother, Hohenlinden Spears, the twin of Brandywine, the paternal Spears having been a great student of battles, followed in exhortation, with the repeated wish that his tongue was longer, — an aspiration so imperfectly shared in his behalf by his hearers that they began to sing him down, after the approved method of quelling such intruders; one hymn-tune after another being quickly raised by the chief brethren, the deaf sister on the front line of seats persistently singing them all in her own time, and generally to her favorite tune of "Bonnie Doon," which she enriched with sundry luxurious quavers. At the height of the melody a newly arrived group of women attracted the hospitable attention of Uncle 'Sias.

"This way," he hoarsely whispered, beckoning from the door of the parlor-bedroom to the sisters, who evidently could see but little beyond the range of their imprisoning sunbonnets; and as they hesitated at noticing the seated occupants of the room, he added, explanatorily, "seats on the edge o' the bed." This somnolent invitation was gratefully accepted, and the log-cabin sunbonnets filed in, and took up their places among the stuffy pillows, just as the singers in the outer room were raising the tune, —

> "Shell *I* be kerried toe the skies
>   On flowery beds of ease ?"

The bed had not been unoccupied through the evening. For twenty years, or for half her life, it had been the habitat of Uncle 'Sias's unhappy daughter, Luce. Jilted, or, as her people said, "shabbed," by the young man whom she was to have married, she never held up her head again after the shock of this misfortune, and took her bed, which she had never since left, — living there " as if it belonged to her organism," and finally sinking into such a hapless state that for years past her mental obituary might have been read in that line of the thoughtful poet of rustic life, —

> " She slowly withered, an imbecile mind."

By one of those coincidences that cease to surprise us by the time that middle age has shown us how often they recur in obedience to some mysterious law, the company of that night happened to include another of the weak-hearted cravens in life's warfare; — a man of mature years, who had never been heard to speak since the blow fell that crushed the pride, the hopes, and the affections of his early manhood. No force of entreaties, taunts, or provocations could drag him from the refuge of silence, which he had sought with a sternness of purpose that, like the woman's pitiful cowering away from

human eyes, testified to the narrow conditions
and imperfect development of lives that went
to wreck in the first storm of disaster by which
they were overtaken.

The meeting was conducted in the usual way.
The customary appeals were made from the lead-
ers to the more timid sisters, and to the young
converts, to rise and speak; and the responses
from each class were, in most instances, of an
inaudible brevity. The maturer standard-bear-
ers rose and delivered the set speeches with
which they always graced these occasions; their
several styles being marked by the repetition of
certain texts to which they had acquired a well-
defined right, — sacred quotations that, as was
said of Emerson's prose " 't is," became almost
a personal possession. For instance, the trade-
mark distinguishing Aunt Rooty, the gatherer
and compounder of simples, the Medea of
savory and medicinal drinks, was the text, " Oh,
taste and see how good the Lord is ! " which she
dwelt upon with a sort of professional unction,
as though she were offering some ptisan of
sovereign virtue. And Miss Experience, or
'Speedy Goodspeed, known for her painful and
halting utterance, never failed to wind up her
remarks with the query, " What shall be done
unto thee, O thou false tongue ? " Then there
was the usual burst of gratitude from the "skinch-
ing," or miserly Deacon Handy, who piously

thanked the Lord that he had been saved from
dead works, and whose hopes of justification
must indeed, according to the testimony of his
neighbors, have rested upon faith alone. The
usual element of comedy was furnished by the
flighty speaker, a sister of infirm wits, but
pious intentions, much given to raising her voice
in a high, cracked tone, and detailing her domestic trials with injudicious frankness, closing
with the application of her favorite " varse." to her
house-mates, " And five of them were foolish."
Her example encouraged "Eelly Dick," the feeble-
minded pauper, whose board the town had let
out to Uncle 'Sias as the lowest bidder, to make
his first appearance on any religious platform, —
getting slightly astray in his attempted citation,
" A woman took a maysure of oil, and hid it in
in a maysure of wheat, until the whole was
leavened," but meeting the Elder's frown with
a manly independence, by the declaration, " I
may not repeat it as verbatim as some, but it is
not for this one, nor that one, nor the other one
to say what I shall say in the great congregation ! "   The Elder urged, warned, and ex-
horted, addressing the doubters and inquirers,
reminding them that Satan desired to have
them, and was there among them; that the
spiritual eye might plainly discern him right
down there by the stove ; and that all concerned
should make haste to leave so dangerous a

vicinity for the haven of the anxious seats.
A pause ensued, of appalling length, after which
a sister rose, and with the pious intention of rub-
bing in the Elder's persuasions, quoted her own
experience at a similar crisis, when she " felt as
if glue could n't begin to hold her down half so
fast as Satan did; but she broke away from all
her bad feelings, and got up and spoke, and felt
quite a good deal better for spiting old Satan."

Perhaps these appeals might have met with
the desired response if the attention of the
young people had not been divided between
ghostly warnings and skyey threatenings.   The
rain, which had been so long gathering in force,
was now preluded by keen flashes of lightning,
and ominous mutterings of thunder.   Seeing
that no movement was made by the objects of
the recent exhortations, Uncle 'Sias rose, just to
occupy the time, as he explained.   " Alas, alas,"
he began, with his highest aim at a conventional
style, "there was a time of blessed news, when
the Lord did marvels amongst us, and we
should rej'ice, yea, and did rej'ice.   But, alas,
the gold is become dim, and the most fine gold
is changed.   Although I hope the' is some
movings on the minds of some few, yit the
saints air not so zeelous f'r the Lord's cause an'
the good o' souls ez they was in times past.
Sin doth greedily abound amongst us, and the
love of many waxes cold, for which the Lord is

angered with a great anger. Now is plantin'
time, in a worldly way o' speakin', but ef we
fare ez we desarve, what sorter harvest shell we
hev? Brethring, it'll be ez it was in times I
knowed when I lived up to Westfield, on Widder
Bacon's farm, when the Lord sent His armies o'
worms to cut off the fruits o' the airth. Thet
season it come 'round so thet they ez expected
fifty bushels did n't git sca'cely one. Seth Beebe
was one of our gret farmers up thet way. He
sowed fo'teen acres o' new ground, an' anticipated on a gret crop. Wal, he plowed it up,
an' planted it with corn. Oh, thet we, ez a
people, rememberin' these jedgments o' times
past, should beware lest they be let loose in the
land agin. Oh, my young frien's we'm all a
lookin' ter you. Oh, think o' the famine in
Egypt; think o' the plagues o' the land; think
o' the good-will o' the burnin' bush; think —"

But here the worthy man's words were lost
in the fierce rush of the gust, the roll of the
thunder, and the maddened lashing of the rain.
Hysterical women, whose twitching shoulders
and quivering chins had for the last quarter of
an hour betrayed their nervous agitation, covered their faces before the blue, blinding lights
that glared pitilessly in at the great uncur-
tained windows of the old farmhouse, and sobbed
in the abject misery of terror. Stout-hearted
Aunt Freelove was heard declaring, "Kind of an

onseasonable sorter thunder-tempest, but I guess
I c'n weather it tell the sullar walls ketches fire."
But Brandywine Spears, who had hitherto sat in
the seat of the scorners, beside the open house
door, now hastily joined the inner circle, a pallid
and crestfallen Mephistopheles, as the racking
peals shook the giant timbers of the room, and
the furious beating of the rain on the roof was
like the tramp of a charging host, while a long,
lurid dazzle, a roar that seemed to fill the sky,
and the sickening sound of a rending, tearing
concussion proclaimed that one of the trees of
the surrounding forest had fallen.   Suddenly,
at this crisis of awe, the mood of the people
passed at once from the ecstacy of fear to the
ecstacy of devotion; a change effected by the
sign and voice of one among them who now
assumed the place of a leader.   At the signal
of this strange, tall hermit figure, known as the
solitary dweller in the centre of the haunted
Carr's Plain, they rose by one impulse to their
feet, and poured out their swelling hearts in a
wild burst of sacred song, their voices mounting
high in the passionate cry of the triumphant
refrain, —

> " Oh, Moses smote the waters,
> And the seas gave way ! "

With the singing of the hymn the tempest
somewhat abated, as if to the clang of mediæval
bells.   Angry black clouds still rose fast from

the ocean, but the lightning glanced harmlessly
through the protecting veil of falling waters, and
the house seemed an ark of safety in the midst
of the raging floods.   All looks now turned
upon the new guide of the evening's devotions,
as he remained standing in his place, with the
abstracted look of a solitary, and yet as if
charged with the burden of a word that must
make its way to utterance.   Unknown and almost nameless as he was to the listening crowd,
there was a power in his presence, in the sug-
gestions of his emaciated countenance and the
spectral glitter of his eye, which pointed to a
reality in the vague background of rumor which
had given him, at his coming to live in their
community, the repute of a seer of strange visions, and of a fearless host to such ghostly visi-
tants as the inhabitants of the haunted territory
which he had chosen to make his dwelling-
place.   But if a suspicion of something un-
hallowed had at first clung to his mysterious
personality, it disappeared with that fuller
knowledge of his brooding enthusiasm, his
meditative insight, and his recondite learning
which had gained him his common title of
"The Preacher," though his voice had never
yet been heard in these seasons of worship.   A
lonely settler in strange places, like the spiritual
fathers of Rhode Island, — Williams, Blackstone,
and Gorton, — it was rumored that he, too,

claimed to be a witness to a special interpretation of sacred truths, and, like those historic
pioneers, had been separated by the stress of
conflicting opinions from his earlier associates,
or, as it was more darkly hinted, had, at the
Divine pleasure, as made known to him in a
dream, left home and family and friends to
dedicate himself to the contemplative life.

Such were the confused ideas prevailing
among the congregation concerning the strange
recluse who now spoke to them, wearing a far-
away, introverted look, which presently quickened and glowed, as his low and quiet tones
grew in intensity with the development of his
theme.

"It is written," he said, without preamble or
address, "in the Word of God that in the last
days He will pour out His spirit upon His servants and hand-maidens, and old men shall
dream dreams, and young men shall see visions.
I had been writing a letter to a friend at a distance, and being weak and feeble, I lay down on
my bed, with my face toward the wall, to take
repose, and soon fell into a sound sleep. Me-
thought I cast my eyes toward heaven, and saw
the blue vault of heaven split asunder, through
which, I thought, I saw a stream of light and
love proceeding from the throne of God, clear
as crystal. As the rays of the sun in the firma-
ment, at its first rising, shine into a door or

window, so that the stream through the whole house will be lighter than anywhere else, so the whole stream of light from heaven to where I stood shined with light and love."

The storm was subsiding, and the flashes of lightning were few and distant, faintly illuminating the horizon. The dreaming glances of the speaker wandered out upon the night, and returned kindled with a deeper light, as he offered a newly-suggested image to his rapt listeners.

"Never did I see anything so straight, and on either side the stream was decked with thousands of little rays of light, all pointing one way, even toward heaven. I thought that every drop of light and love that God bestows is to be returned to Him again; and while I stood wondering at the sight, I thought I saw the fiery chariot of God's love come through the gap that was in the vault, coming through the midst of the stream, a hundred times swifter than I ever saw an eagle fly. I thought it was all over glorious, and in color like to a rainbow, and was carried on wings of love. In a few moments it was just by where I stood, and turned short about, with the fire part toward heaven, and rested on its wings, keeping its wings in a slow motion to bear it up, and waiting for me to come in. I thought my soul was transported; I thought I stood with my heart and hands extended to heaven, crying, Glory, glory in the highest! and just as I was about to mount into the chariot I turned to a great multitude, crying, Glory, glory, I am going to glory in the fiery chariot of His love! and with these words on my lips I awoke out of sleep. Oh, cried I, in tears, that I had been suffered to take my flight! Oh, thought I, in the bitter disappointment of those waking moments, if one view of glory and love will fill a soul with such joy, even in a dream, what will the open vision and full fruition be in glory?"

The preacher's voice broke and failed, the light died out of his wan face, his Dantean vision was told, his mission was ended. The message that he had delivered was in a tone of fervor and power so far above the usual spiritual ministrations received by the flock that a confused sense of wonder sat upon all the faces. But the Elder, or exhorter of the evening, catching something of the enthusiast's emotion, dismissed them with the genuine dignity of a pastoral guide.

"Brethren," said he, "our brother has spoke to us in the word of power. As we go to our homes, and lay us down to rest, let us meditate well thereupon; and let each one commune with his own heart, and be still." And he gave, and the congregation received, a blessing, with a new sense of reverence.

As the people disappeared on their homeward ways the sky was still obscured by drifting fog, through which glimpses of the clear heavens, set with star-points, promised a further April change to fair weather. But the atmosphere of storm and cloud and mist has ever since hung so heavily over the story of that night that it has finally come to wear the shadowy shape of a legend of the South County.

L OUISA, Mrs. Gould's young daughter, was
ailing with an indisposition that had not as
yet assumed any definite form, though some of
her symptoms were thought to point to lung
fever, or "side-anguish."

The invalid was not left to pine in solitude.
In the kitchen-bedroom, which she temporarily
occupied, were her aunt, old Miss Esther, or
Eesther Gould, Friend Mahala Clark, otherwise
"Cousin M'hal'," who was neighboring with them
for the day, and whose distant relationship was
made the means of a compromise between a
" Friendly" and a worldly form of addressing a
person of years and dignity, — with the juvenile
Gid Gould, whom a sprained ankle detained at
home, and who resorted to his sister's room in
restless search after some acceptable indoor en-
tertainment. Added to these sources of companionship was the near presence of several
children of the village, who had gathered in the
door-yard, and, surrounding one of their number
placed in the centre of the circle, were shouting
at her the rhymed salutation of their game, —

"Queen Anne, Queen Anne, she sits in the sun,
    As fair as a lady, as bright as a nun."

In the intervals of their song some anony-
mous crying, which might safely be credited
to one at least of the five babies in the imme-
diate neighborhood, was pleasantly borne on
the breeze, or the frail and precarious pipe of
a solitary fowl, just under the sick-room window, made itself hoarsely heard, in the gloomy
monosyllable "kurk," or the prolonged groan
"kur-*ruck*," uttered with a moving melancholy
that might well make converts to the Pytha-
gorean doctrine expounded by the clown in
"Twelfth Night," that the soul of our grandam
might haply inhabit a bird, and convince them
that this pathetic Dame Partlet was the identical
fowl.

" I do b'lieve that faowl's hungry," was Aunt
Eesther's more practical interpretation of a few
notes of this mournful music; "she never come
round when the rest on 'em was fed, f'r I see
her a-sottin' thiar all the time. Gid, jest you
shell out a han'ful o' them ears a-hangin' up
thiar. Here, coop, coop, coop! Good land!
how the cretur dooz gaffle it down!" cackled
the good old dame, whose voice and laugh were
as quaintly thin and sharp as the vibrant shrilling
of insects.

Aunt Eesther repaired the ravages of age by
the friendly aid of a cap and a black "foretop,"

over which she oddly wore the brown satin
snood of her youth, on the principle that it
was as good as ever it was, and had ought to
be wore out. Her scant gown and the little
shawl she had crossed over her chest assimi-
lated her general appearance to that of Friend
Clark; but the latter was neater, nicer, and wore
her plain gown with a sort of refined rusticity.
The lappets of her clear-starched cap, of "sheer"
muslin, fell to her shoulders, and her spectacles
shed benevolent lights as they mildly beamed
on the invalid.

The latter was a delicate girl of twenty, of
the usual transitory type of pale prettiness so
often seen in the homes and schools of New
England. She had the softness and freshness
of contour and complexion that make the inevitable beauty of youth, always so lightly
regarded by its possessor, and never appreciated until regretted. But she had not the
grace of youth, for her thin, tall figure, and
high shoulders, gave her an invalid look, even
in her firmest health. Now, however, as she
rested against the folds of the coarse, brown
cottons, which many washings had partially
bleached and softened from their first crude
estate, her dark hair and eyes, and her clear-
toned coloring assumed their full value; and
her looks, if they had been cheerful, would
have been of supreme charm; for her fever

was as yet only of that incipient type which brightens the eye and flushes the check with a hectic counterfeit of the triumph of high health.

"Don't ye feel now ez ef ye could n't eat no dinner, Loweyezy?" questioned her aunt with unintentional ambiguity.

"The' was fowl-pie, with quohogs in it f'r dinner," volunteered Gid, with appropriate enthusiasm.

"Could n't thee eat some of the bread-kind, Leeweeza?" benevolently queried Friend Clark.

The invalid declined this cereal feast, and with the restlessness of increasing fever, turned impatiently in bed.

"Here comes the Clacksum girls," proclaimed Aunt Eesther with animation. "Now thet's fort'nit; like ez not they'm brung ye some relish f'r y'r supper. They ain't never killed yit, — it's too airly yit awhile ter be tryin' out leaf lard, — but some hog's pluck is jest what folks kinder wants now, ain't it? Some liver, now, — "

> "Eat the liver, live forever;
> Eat the lights, die to rights,"

vociferated Gid, flinging himself on his sister's bed, as the guests entered.

The three Clacksum girls, Phyluty, Pashe (from Patience), and Osey (or Osianna), belonged to that numerous class whose girlhood is prolonged by a fashion of speech to the

furthest possible point.   But they must be ac-
quitted of any intention to profit by this benefit
of courtesy, for Phyluty, always the spokes-
woman of the group, addressing the sick girl
in a loud voice, and with a lively sniff, both well
adapted to cheer her depressed spirits, informed
her "that she'd haf to get well right away now,
sence the old maids had got round to see her at
last."   This humorous description of herself
was Phyluty's perennial joke, and her acquaintances were expected to find perpetual mirth in
it.   Having been in the habit of steadily regarding it, for the last twenty years and more, as an
excellent merry jest, she seemed now either to
ignore or to forget the more serious aspects of
the case, as it presented itself to an observer;
so that she afforded an instructive instance of
that curious tendency of the individual to make
light of the supposed privations of humanity;
for nothing is more common than to hear the
solitary, the childless, the sickly, and the aged
jesting at their condition in life, not, with simple
folk, from any definite motive of pride or self-
assertion, but from a confused, instinctive
prompting toward adjustment to one's environ-
ment.   And even among people of a more
complex self-consciousness, you shall hear
women making sprightly allusions to their old-
maidhood, and men dwelling with humorous
touches upon their advancing years, seemingly

unaware that, to the mere matter-of-fact observer, both subjects have long passed "the limits of becoming mirth."

Osey, the third sister, who had inherited sundry peculiar traits that differentiated her from the commonplace order of mind, had perfected an ingenious scheme for fastening a desperate clutch upon receding Time; and by always stating her age at an advance of seven years beyond what it really was, enjoyed the questionable refreshment of being called quite a young-looking woman — of her age.

" I thought I 'd fetch Leeweezy some dangle-berries," observed Phyluty, in modest reference to the contents of her mysterious little basket. " Ye see they 'm gittin' ter be a kind of a sc'ace yarb now, an' I did n't know but what they 'd taste good to her."

" Loweyezy don't never eat 'em," frankly responded Aunt Eesther, with the uncompromising truthfulness of country breeding, " but we 'm obleeged ter ye, jest the same."

"Well now, I allers was a gret hand f'r sass out o' season," remarked Pashe, reflectively.

" Yes," agreed Phyluty, that leading lady of the social comedy, " I dono 's you reck'lect the time Pashe had a poor spell, — kind of a fall fever, — an' the' wa'n't nothin' 't she took a notion t' eat, 'nless 't was some red rozbries. Well, we did n't say nothin', but Osey, she scurried

round, an' 't las' she come in one day 'n' said ter
Pashe, 'Which hand 'll you take, the right or the
left?' 'Sho!' says Pashe, ''t ain't red rozbries,
I know; red rozbries hes abeout subsided.'
'Well, they 'm very good *eatin'* rozbries anyway,'
says I, 'ef they ain't so harnsum ez the airly
ones;' f'r ye see, they was the fall kind.   An'
Pashe begun ter pick up right away after that, so
't she never missed a meal."

Phyluty concluded her narrative with an effective sniff.   This mode of expression was one
that she had nearly brought to perfection, and
there were few notes in the gamut of her emotions that could not be rendered by some modi-
fication of this energetic facial action.

The invalid again moved wearily on her pil-
low, and Aunt Eesther hastened to smooth its
folds, with the mild reminder, —

"Folks could n't never say of you, Lowcyezy,
ez they uster say of Cousin M'hal', thet she
would be the sickest woman, an' yit keep the
smoothest bed-clothes, 't ever they see."

" Thee feels distressed, Leeweeza," said Cousin
M'hal', with a subdued expression of kindliness,
answering to the frank smile of affection which
lights up the unchastened lineaments of the
world's people, and speaking in tones steeped
in some source of inexhaustible calm, " but thee
will learn, as thee lives along, to bear pain an'
tortur."

"Leeweezy's Cousin Rit went off suddin, to the last, didn't she?" plaintively inquired Oscy, who naturally felt the propriety of confining the conversation strictly to edifying sick-room topics. "You an' she was jest of an age, an' you was allers very *great*, wa'n't you, Leeweezy?" she pursued, with a glance at the bed; to which statement its occupant mutely assented. "I uster think she was tougher 'n' any pitch-knot; she wa'n't one o' the kind that never makes old bones" — with another glance at the invalid, "not ter look at her, she wa'n't; an' she wa'n't one o' them that hes sick spells; but she giv' way all ter onct."

Pashe now took up the thread of conversation so deftly spun by the sisters three, affirming that she "never see no poor cretur that seemed to take things so patient and resigned as Ritty did. She told Elder Fowler what text she'd have preached from when he buried her, and she picked out all of her bearers, and they said she seemed real distressed for fear 't would n't be a good day for her funeral, after she'd planned it all out so. They said she was a beautiful planner of a funeral."

"Yes; she was composed in her mind," emphatically pronounced Phyluty, with a meaning sniff; "she was a beautiful girl." This latter tribute to the departed, who had had the misfortune to be of singular personal plainness, was of course

understood to refer to that moral loveliness
which affords the only ideal of beauty recognized in the rustic colloquialisms of feminine
New England.

"*He* ain't here, is he?" inquired Osey, with
apparent irrelevance, and nodding in the direction of Louisa.

".No," hesitated Aunt Eesther, with the awk-
wardness of a person totally unused to practise
reserve on any topic; "ye see"— hurriedly —
"he's got work now, way off to Biscuit City,
an' he's up there a lathin', an' Loweyezy, she's ,
come home to her own folks, ter stay a spell.
I expect, though, she misses her ma, now she's
took sick."

"Mis' Gould hes gone to her sister's, ain't
she?" continued the anxious inquirer.

"Yes, ye know she's got a young baby, an'
her hands is tied, so 't she's all behind with
her work, an' she begun ter shake in her shoes
fer fear she would n't be through house-cleanin'
afore the thrashers come. An' then they'd haf
ter kill next, an' nobody but her ter do a hand's
turn, an' she's all overdone with ev'rything
hangin' by the eyelids so."

Osey opined that she must have just about as
much as she could fly under; and, after a few
further expressions of neighborly interest, and
not a few tokens of neighborly inquisitiveness,
the sisters rose, apparently to go, but really, as

it proved, to stand for the space of some long
minutes, while Pashe, who had just bethought
herself of a sovereign charm against illness, related, with some assistance from Osey, chiefly
bestowed in the form of vigorous corrections of
her narrative, the process of cutting off a lock
of a sick person's hair in the increase of the
moon, and pinning it to the wall, so that the
moonlight should rest on it every night for a
week, after which time the invalid would begin
to improve; though, to be sure, as she concluded, there was n't no moon just now. Phyluty
was reminded of a case in which this spell had
worked marvels, and proceeded to relate it; but
in so doing, plunged into the intricacies of a colloquial labyrinth, wherein panting print would
toil after her in vain. Speech alone could repro-
duce the repeated " s'e " for " said he," or " said
she," and " s'I " for " said I," with the other frac-
tional currency of social exchange which she
tendered in such profusion that her sisters were
fain to admonish her that her tongue " run like a
ginger-mill." But at last they buzzed themselves
away, as flies will finally go out of an open
door.

   " 'Bijah ! " called Aunt Eesther to a slouching,
shabby man, furtively lounging by, " now while
I think on 't, jest you fetch a pail o' water."

   " Ef the Mississippi River run through this
house 't would n't bring water enough ter satisfy

the durned women-folks," growled the man; but
he finally retraced his steps, with ostentatious
dilatoriness, to do the hated service.

'Bijah Fry, Mrs. Gould's disreputable brother,
who "made his home" with her, or was tolerated as an unwelcome housemate during the
tedious intervals between his precarious "jobs,"
had long cherished a jealous grudge against
harmless Aunt Eesther, both as the helpful and
valued dependent of the two inmates of the family, and as the energetic contriver of "chores"
and "arrants," the execution of which fell to
him. He was not the less irritable for having
but lately returned from a prolonged "clam-
ming" with sundry associates whose habits were
well known to be more convivial than industrial.
As he again passed the window Aunt Eesther
put out her head and quavered, —

"Where be ye a-goin' now, 'Bijah?" bringing
him face to face with her as he snapped, —

"Right straight to —— [they did n't say *sheol*
then], Eest'; don't yer wanter send an arrant?"

"Ef the' was any shame in ye, 'Bijah Fry,
yer 'd be ashamed ter gin sech an' arnswer when
I wanted ye ter fetch the doctor," returned the
indignant old lady, femininely oblivious of the
fact that her purpose had remained undeveloped.

"Why did n't ye say so, then?" angrily
sneered her quasi brother-in-law, with a disgust
that equalled her own. "I 'd a done it for *her*,"

he added, with a touch of genuine concern in his manner, as he looked in at the sick girl. "I'll do it willin'ly," he loudly resumed, with swelling dignity, and indulging in a gloating animosity, "f'r any poor gal, let alone my own niece, es hes got the misfortin' ter have a stiff-necked lunkhead f'r a husband, a reg'lar she-boss f'r a mother-in-law, an' ole Eesther Gould f'r a nuss."

Louisa looked pained by this rude championship, and the feverish flush mounted to her forehead, but she said nothing.

"'Bijah must ha' swallered old razors, he's so mighty sharp," scornfully commented Aunt Eesther.

"'Bijah, thee *is* a trial," sighed the Friend, looking after the retreating swagger of his disreputable figure. "He makes me think," she continued, "of the old man that went everywhere asking for work, and praying that he might not find it. Did thee hear, Eesther, how he come over the other day when I was busy with my molasses-quince, doing up the skins and cores. Thee knows the deeper in his cups 'Bijah gets the more solemn-wayed he is, and he said he come to me with a message from the Lord to convert me and my house to the Methodist way. His coat-pockets was all weighted down with Methodist books — where dooz thee suppose he got them? — and don't thee think," pursued the Friend, with mild protest, "he wanted me to bring him all of Friends' publications that brother Amram keeps in his book-closet, and sit down and listen to him while he read out loud, and compared them with his books. I never was so put by, and I told him, 'Thy zeal is not according to knowledge, 'Bijah; thee pesters me;' but just then husband come in and got him to go up to the lot and see what he thought of the sick colt; for thee knows, Eesther, 'Bijah used to be a man of good judgment, and a forcible man, when he was himself."

"No, I dono's I ever knowed no good on him," replied Aunt Eesther, with pardonable resentment.

"Miss Esther Protester was sent to the Queen,
The most modish young lady that ever was seen,"

repeated Gid, who was occasionally seized with a desire to take part in the social exercise of the afternoon.

"Was that air writ about you, Aunt Eesther?"

"Lor', no, child," affably returned his relative, "but I've heerd it amongst the old folks here, time out o' mind."

"The's some more on it," persisted Gid, "where it says, —

"'Is Miss Esther within, or is she without?
No, she's up chamber, a-walkin' about.'"

"Yes, yes," nodded Aunt Eesther, "I've

knowed it ever sence I was a teenty tawnty
gal."

"Then what's that other one?" continued
Master Gid, charmed to find his overtures received with more than wonted consideration,
"you know thet one about the old keow —

"'What kin ye do with the old keow's hoof?
'T will make ez good a shingle ez ever teched roof.
What kin ye do with the old keow's head?
'T will make ez good an oven ez ever baked bread;
White bread, or brown bread, or any sich a thing —'"

"Does thee like thy schooling, Gid?" pleasantly asked Friend Clark, by way of timely
diversion.

"Like 't well 'nough, most times," graciously
replied the youth. "Frid'y fortnits is the wust
on it. Makes me sick ter hear the girls get off
their compositions. Our school's chock full o'
nat'ral fools — mostly girls — " generalized the
young philosopher. "Ev'ry one on 'em writes
a letter, an' ev'ry one on 'em gets up jest as
mincin' — so fashion," — as he attempted an
illustration, — "an' sweetens up her voice, an'
reads out, 'I go to school to Miss Ann Scranton,
which I like ve-ry much.'" Gid mimicked the
small girlish pipe with impatient disgust. "They
don't no such a thing! They don't like old Ann
Scran any better 'n I do."

"Why dooz n't thee like thy kind teacher?"
gently inquired the good Friend.

" 'Cause she wears them brass thimbles on her ten fingers, an' cracks you over the head when you ain't lookin'," promptly explained the youth.

" And what dooz the boys say in their letters?" further queried Friend Clark, abandoning the defence of the amiable teacher.

" The boys don't write," returned Gid, with contempt. " Them 's f'r girls. The boys speaks pieces. Si Bently hed ' The Seasons,' an' s'e, ' Some like spring, some like winter best; but ez f'r me, give me libbaty or give me death!' "

" Was thy teacher pleased then?"

" No; he got kep' arter school. She said 't was too short," Gid added, with a musing air.

" 'Nother time," he resumed, brightening up, " Si got up ter speak, an' s'e, ' Friends, Romans, Countrymen, and Lovers, lend me yer ears. Mother 's gonter bile souse ter-morrer, an' wants ter git all she kin.' "

" Did thy teacher punish him for such wrong conduct? "

" Guess she did," grinned Gid, with retrospective delight. Then, interrupting his recital of the trials of this unappreciated humorist, he announced: " Say, I b'lieve I c'n make out ter hobble roun' some now," and disappeared in the direction of the garret stairs, whence he presently returned with a struggling cat, a penknife, and a large spool. The relations between these three objects became more apparent as he began the process of shaving the tip of the cat's tail in order to string the spool firmly upon it.

"Say, Gid, what *be* you a-doin'?" asked Louisa, with annoyance.

"Hey, whossay?" automatically replied the youth, whose attention was anxiously centred upon the threatening mews — not loud, but deep — of the afflicted animal.

"I say, what does make you cruelize that poor dumb cretur so?" repeated his sister with invalid fretfulness.

"Wal, 't ain't ourn," answered Gid, convincingly. "She's a wile-cat. She ain't dumb, neither. Wisht she was. (Buhstill thiar! can't ye buhstill?) Ketched her down 't the brook when I was lookin' up turkles. Come on to her all cajunk. She scratched 'n' sung some, same 's she does now — Scat! ye most went through my thumb!" — and as Gid applied that injured member to his mouth puss with one frantic effort writhed herself from his grasp, and in a single leap cleared the window; while her tormentor gazed after her in keen disappointment.

"Uhdone, Gideon Gould!" sternly menaced Aunt Eesther, adding the mysterious nautical threat, "Uhdone, or I'll cleave ye from clue ter earring! Mr. Pillsbury 's comin' in."

After this manner Aunt Eesther, like others of

her class, commonly described and addressed a doctor.

The village doctor of that day was a taciturn, routine-plodding " drugger," as he was sometimes not inappropriately called. The old saddle-bags — which now accompanied him in his wagon, since he no longer went his rounds on horseback — were loaded to bursting with the heaviest ammunition used in the warfare of the medical profession with the insurgent forces of disease. He wore a wig that might have seen better days among the many it had evidently known; and his coat was as splashed and stained with traces of rough riding as if he had been a king's messenger. The old white steed that had made many roundabout journeys in the township, and which had partly earned for his rider the title of " Death on the Pale Horse," stood contentedly cropping the roadside grass.

Louisa shrank with the morbid sensitiveness of her acutely nervous temperament from his business-like look and touch; but he coolly ignored his patient, addressing most of his inquiries to her aunt, and muttered at intervals to himself as if he were composing an incantation wherewith to exorcise the evil spirit of illness.

" Her skin feels dreadful fevery, Doctor," ventured the old woman, who stood anxiously awaiting his commands. " I expect she 's overdone, an' she 's kep' up too long. Ye see, she 's got

too much resolution, an' so she's run down all
to onct, an'—"

"Sho, nonsense!" vouchsafed the great man.
"She needs to get blooded, that's all. Bring
me the bowl!"

Obedient to the expected mandate, Aunt Eesther presently returned, bearing the bowl, and
looking like a rustic Muse of Tragedy; while the
Doctor, quick with his lancet, opened a vein in
the slender arm of the trembling girl.

"That'll do," he magisterially announced,
after a shorter interval of silent attention than was
usually allotted to this familiar form of surgery,
speaking in a tone in which contempt and toleration, with a certain relenting toward the youth,
sex, and nervous distress of his patient were
curiously blended,—"that's all, Louisa. Sha'n't
bleed her much. A flea-bite knocks her over.
S' got no staminy."

With this frank statement the Doctor proceeded to portion out the drugs to be adminis-
tered in the night, and was leaving with the
assurance that he would be 'round in the morning, when Aunt Eesther, curiously smelling and
tasting one of the doses, must needs delay him
to ask,—

"What's this here you'm gi'n her, Mr. Pillsbury? I don't seem ter make 't out egzac'ly."

"That is *medicine*, marm!" shouted the en-
raged physician in no sick-room voice.

"The land, Mr. Pillsbury! I never laid out ter affront ye," began Aunt Eesther; but he was already out of hearing.

"Deary me!" panted the worthy old lady, "he's dreadful crickery, ain't he? Loweyczy, how d' ye feel now? Powerful weak, ain't ye, arter that bleedin'? Wal, I wisht Cousin M'hal' could a sot with ye a spell longer; but she tho't she mus' go when 't come sunset.

> "'When Darby see the settin' sun
> He slung his sy', an' home he run,'"

repeated Aunt Eesther, who sometimes adorned her discourse with poetical fragments.

"Lor', you uster be jest crazy to hev me tell ye them varses in blindman's holiday same 's 't is now. My poor old mem'ry 's mos' wore out," she continued with a meek show of depreciation that decently veiled her harmless vanity; "but I guess I could worry through with 'The Three Warnin's.'"

No response from the patient.

"Or else," this all-accomplished nurse volunteered, "thiar 's 'William an' Marg'ret,' yer know.

> "'When all was wrapt in dark midnight,
> And all were fast asleep,
> In glided Margaret's grimly ghost,
> And stood at William's feet.'"

A slight movement and a faint sigh of weariness reached Aunt Eesther's sympathetic ear.

"Wal, 't is kinder pokerish," she admitted;
" an' so 's ' Alonzo the Brave and the Fair Imo-
gene; ' but you allers was dreadful fond o'
' Barbry Allen.' "

And Aunt Eesther, with infinite relish, and
rocking back and forth in time to the arbitrary
emphasis which she gave to sundry words, repeated, —

> " In Scarlet *town* where I was *born*,
> There was a fair *maid* dwelling,
> Made every youth cry, Wel-away !
> .   Her *name* was Barbara *Allen*."

The invalid grew restless long before her
quaint companion had reached the climax of
the narrative, —

> "He turned his face unto the wall
> As deadly pangs he fell in ;
> Adieu, adieu, adieu to all !
> Adieu to Barbara Allen !
>
> As she was walking o'er the fields
> She heard the bells a-knelling,
> And every stroke did seem to say,
> Unworthy Barbara Allen !
>
> .   .   .   .   .   .
>
> With scornful eye she looked down,
> Her cheek with laughter swelling;
> Whilst all her friends cried out amain,
> Unworthy Barbara Allen !
>
> When he was dead and laid in grave,
> Her heart was struck with sorrow ;
> O mother, mother, make my bed,
> For I shall die to-morrow !

> Hard-hearted creature him to slight
>> Who lovéd me so dearly!
> O that I had been more kind 'to him
>> When he was alive and near me!

> She, on her death-bed as she lay,
>> Begged to be buried by him "—

"Don't, Aunt Eesther, don't!" sobbed the girl with a sudden violence that seemed to emanate from some deeper source of emotion than physical exhaustion or sympathy with the grotesque sentiment of the old ballad; then struggling hard for self-control, she begged, "Please, don't! It makes me so nervous!"

"There, there, child!" patiently responded the kindly old dame. "Why did n't ye say so afore? My pity! yer all wore out, ain't ye? There now, jest yer wait tell I put some mustard drafts ter yer feet an' gin ye some o' yer soothin' mixtur', an' mebbe ye 'll feel better."

These offices concluded, and the patient lying still in a sort of tense quietude, the silence of the dimly-lighted room was again broken by a soft though measured foot-fall, and the subdued sound of a kind voice asking pleasantly, "How does Leeweeze seem ter be now?"

"Char*lotte* Temple!" exclaimed the old lady, starting up from her doze, and, according to her custom, addressing the welcome guest, Widow Wilson, by her "given name" in full, "I'm a thousan' times obleeged ter ye fer comin'! I

tole her par when he come back 'n' said yer 'd
be here ter-night thet I was bounden ter ye 'nough
sight. I expect Loweyezy's be'n frettin' her head
off fer ye all day. I dono 's she railly needs a
watcher; but yer 'll be comp'ny f'r her, an'
there 's lots o' med'cine ter give. *I*'m an old
woman, Char*lotte*," impressively proclaimed
Aunt Eesther, — who apparently still harbored
that subtle conviction which dies so hard in
the feminine consciousness, that the fact of age
never becomes patent to observers unless duly
announced, — " an' it stan's to reason 't I can't
be on my feet night 'n' day. I be'n on the go
sence four o'clock, an' I 'm putty well wagged ;
'Bijah he 's be'n a-tewin' roun', an' Gid he 's
be'n inter mischief, an' I arter 'em, an' when
I wrung out my dish-clout ter-night I was
eenemost ready ter drop."

The widow, with the quiet efficiency of experience, began looking over the medicines.

" That 's the doze-powder," explained Aunt
Eesther.

" Dover's powder," interjected the patient.

" Wal, 't 's all one, ain't it ? " returned the aunt
in a tone of quasi injury. " Lor', when Loweyezy's
a leetle grain crickery, she 'll grammarize ev'ry
word 't I speak! An' this here 's the sweet
nitre, an' this stuff in the cup," shaking it sus-
piciously — " no, I dono what 't is. Mr. Pillsbury mos' took my head off f'r axin' him a civil

question. I dono what ailed him; but they
say he was a dretful crosspatch when he was a
baby, an' I guess he hain't never outgrowed it.
Wal, good-night ter both on ye. Guess I sh'll
sleep 'thout rockin' ter-night. Char*lotte* [to the
widow, who had followed her into the kitchen],
I'm real glad yer come; she thinks the world on
ye; an' I'm afeered she's dretful slim; she wa'n't
never real rugged. Wal, I've eenemost watched
myself! It's nigh on ter ten o'clock now!"

"Yer don't *look* so dreadful sick, Leeweeze,"
said Charlotte, reassuringly, on her return. "I've
heard tell of folks thet was so homely they hed
ter hev watchers: but yer don't look that way."

"Oh, Charlotte!" panted the suffering girl,
whose fever had now returned with violence; "I
do feel so fevery! Raise me up; give me a
drink o' water."

"I dursn't, child," sorrowfully replied her
friend. "The doctor said yer could hev *some*
water, — a teaspoonful to a time. Well, there,"
as her patient's distress increased, "I'll resk it
f'r yer ter drink thet much in the cup; but yer
be a good girl, an' don't ask f'r no more now.
Poor child!" as the girl fell back with a shuddering sigh; "yer miss y'r mother, an' yer miss
Jim, don't yer?"

"Oh, Charlotte!" cried the sufferer as this
firm touch probed her morbid consciousness,
"Yer know all about it, then?"

11

"I know nothin' more 'n I see when I come inter this room," returned the other. "I see y'r heart was full quick 's as I set eyes on yer. But don't yer talk now; yer c'n tell me some other time, an' nef yer want to."

"No; I must, I must tell yer now," cried the young creature, wildly, her pent-up passion finding voice at last.

"Well, I don't never let none o' my sick folks go ter talkin'," hesitated the new nurse, divided in judgment as to her patient's most pressing needs; then yielding to the appeal that looked so cravingly from the dark eyes, she said, "Well, talk a little while ef yer want, an' then mebbe yer 'll sleep better when yer git it off y'r mind. Jest yer let me fix the clo'es 'round ye an' straighten ye out a little. There, there, now," murmured the elder woman as if to a child, taking one of the throbbing wrists between her cool, soothing palms.

"Oh, I know I 've done bad," began the girl, in tearless wretchedness, "but it all begun little by little, an' who would thought 't would come ter this in sca'cely mor 'n a year's time!"

"Yer mean yer an' Jim has hed fallin's out?" quietly asked her companion, with a penetration that astonished the inexperience of the younger woman.

"Yes, oh yes; I would n't care about no sickness ef only I felt right in my mind; but

I expect the way I took sick in the first place
was becos I worried an' cried so."

"But how come ye ter leave yer husband,
Leeweeze? Could n't ye fix things right, noway? I never sh'd tho't yer'd been so uppish
that yer could n't get along with folks."

"Oh, I could n't stan' it no longer with
Mother Flint," cried the girl, with an air of
challenge. "Yer don't begin ter know what
she's like. She's a reg'lar born scold. Mebbe
she can't help it, — Jim says she can't, — an'
I don't wish her a speck o' harm, an' ef she
was sick I'd wait on her, an' tend on her; but,
Charlotte, I ain't got the grace ter live with
her day in an' day out. She's dreadful hard
ter live with; her own folks says so. Her
daughter uster get so worked up when she
was ter home that she'd fling right out before
the neighbors, an' say, 'I think my mother's
the worst woman in the world!' Ev'rybody
says she fretted Mr. Flint inter his grave, an'
how could I expect to hold up my sides with
her? She faulted me for ev'rything I did, an'
ev'rything I did n't do, tell I got so nervious
I was fairly 'fraid o' the shadder o' her sun-
bunnit hangin' up against the wall."

"Sho, Leeweeze, that was real silly."

"Well, I do suppose I was jest the worst one
to hev went there; I wa'n't one thet could
give her back ez good ez I got, an' yet I wa'n't

one o' the kind ter be put upon an' never say
Ah! Yes? nor No! I wa'n't real patient an'
pleased with her, — I dono who could be,
'nless 't was the deef 'n' dumb. So she giv'
me no peace, tell at larst I got ter bein' pretty
nigh ez highstrung ez she was, an' then she
was sooted, becos she could leave off talkin'
about my sulks, an' talk about my tempers.
That galled Jim, I knew; fer he could n't
never enjure women thet was coarse-wayed
and tonguey. I s'pose he 'd hed enough of '
it ter home, an' he liked me becos he thought
I was quiet an' pretty-wayed. Well, thet 's all
over, now. And then they 'd always made a
poppet of me, here ter home, an' Ma kep' put-
tin' me up ter things; an' when I 'd tell her
how I fared with Mother Flint, she 'd say she 'd
take my part, ef Jim would n't. An' thet was
ez true a word ez ever was spoke; he would n't
take no sides; seemed ter think my troubles
was too small business fer him, altogether. He
said he knew enough ter keep outer all women
fights, an' it made me feel ill towards him ter
see how he looked down on me, fer complainin'
the least mite. Ef I named his mother's name
ter him, it madded him, an' he 'd say he mus'
go right off an' weed the garding, though I
knew well 'nough 't wa'n't sufferin'. Charlotte,"
she turned toward her companion, seeking her
face with appealing eyes, "do you b'lieve any-

body ever is ez good ter yer ez yer own folks
be? When I was ter home my folks hed feelin's
fer me, an' set store by me, right along, whether
I done good or done bad; but when yer go
off among other folks, they 'll only treat yer
ez well ez yer 've airned a right ter be treated,
ef they do thet. But I feel real condemned
ter say so, too; fer Jim was kind ez could be,
most o' the time, and he uster get all worked
up when I hed my bad spells. 'Now, sis,' he
uster tell me, 'you must hev the doctor, right
off,' — an' ther' was times when he 'd lose the
heft of a day's work goin' fer him an' gettin'
back, 'sides his charges, an' never say a word
about his wife's bein' nothin' but a bill of ex-
pense, the way Squire Stonan does about his'n;
and he 's a real rich man, an' rides in a wagin,
an' hes his house painted. But Jim would n't
never own thet 't was his mother's hateful ways
thet giv' me my bad headaches; he always
would hev it thet I 'd got cold, or else I 'd et
somethin' thet wa'n't hulsome. He never minds
his mother's talk, no more 'n the wind thet
blows, an' he could n't make out why I did.
So, whatever I 'd tell him, he was dreadful
clus-mouthed, an' would n't take no notice, no
more 'n ef I was jest a mad child. Then I 'd
shet myself up an' cry hours to a time, ter think
how changed he was to-wards me; for when he
was goin' with me, he was quick enough ter

flare up if anybody laid a straw in my path; an' when he took a notion how thet or'nary Joe Harkins only looked kinder onhandsome at me, he follered him afterwards, — so the folks told me, — an' took him ter do fer it, an' when Joe giv' him some impidence, Jim told him, 'You mean dog, you, I'll thrash the ground with you!' An' he did, too."

"Don't yer realize 't yer'll tire yerself all out, talkin' this rate?" interposed her anxious listener.

"I can't stop now, Charlotte," pleaded the sufferer, with a restless impatience to recite the whole unhappy story of her brief wedded life. "I was all overbecome ter fare so with Jim, an' didn't know what ter make of it, fer I'd never thought things would go so hard. You know well 'nough how 't is with Pa. Pa thinks Ma made the world, an' everythin' here goes jes' ez she says. And there's Uncle Samson, — ef he thinks any thoughts, they'm his wife's thoughts; an' what words he speaks is his wife's words; so 't it's real ridic'lous ter hear him lay down the law, when you know all the time it's Aunt Sarah Ann jes' makin' a mouthpiece on him; fer he shets his eyes an' takes her jedgment right along in everythin', from ridge-poles ter cap-borders. I see all thet, an' course I thought, — well, I s'pose I thought I sh'd hev' *some* infl'ence. But the most o' women finds it the

same, I guess; love don't count ter men folks
ez it does ter us; it ain't anythin' thet comes
inter their lives an' drives ev'rythin' else out,
ez it does with us women. Becos a man loved
me, or said he did, I tho't 't was kingdom
come on airth, an' 't I oughter do jest ez he
said, an' so I went ter live with his mother, though
I knew better all the time. But it's diff'rent
with a man somehow. Ef a woman loves him,
why in course she ought ter, — does it becos she
wants ter, anyway. He don't see no partic'lar
meerit ter it, an' no reason 't all why he sh'd everlastin'ly hear ter her on account on' t. Ef she
loves him, why thet's her privilege; he ain't
noways obligated by it.

"But Jim an' me got along well enough, in a
manner o' speakin'; fer the' is times when pride
stan's yer best friend, an' so I wa'n't all the time
hectorin' of him, ez I hev heard women doin',
always askin', ' Say, do yer love me ez much this
Mond'y mornin' ez yer did las' Wednesd'y afternoon?' or full ez foolish ez thet. I always was
disgusted with it, an' I could be contented enough
though Jim did n't make no gret fuss with me, so
long 's I knew 't was jest his queer way. Mostly
't was kinder in joke ef he noticed me an' made
much o' me; fer course he was jest like all the
men folks, forever a-jokin', talkin' every which-
way, an' never gettin' anywhiar. I never see
sech shaller nonsense ez they take fer wit. I

uster say t' him: 'Jim Flint, ef I was you, ef I hed any wit I 'd show it;' an' thet would set him off again worse 'n ever. He 'd say I was very severe on him. I b'lieve jes' what kep' him a funnin' so was becos I never once knowed what under the canopy he meant by any of his comical talk. He uster call me his standin' joke, an' the best joke of all; but I knowed he liked me a sight better for not takin' it all in than ef I 'd be'n one o' them women thet 's so everlastin' smart 't they know the whole story 'fore a man 's got two words on it outer his mouth."

"Then yer an' Jim wa'n't allers at swords' pints, ye see," mildly suggested her friend. "Had n't yer better quiet down a spell now? Jest see how yer fever rages ! "

"Oh, no ! " she scornfully rejected the well-meant warning. "Course we had some frien'ly times. I was always quiet-wayed, an' no gret han' ter make acquaintance or go runnin' in ter the neighbors', so 't I kinder depended on Jim fer most o' the comp'ny I had. But Mother Flint always come between us ; ef she wa'n't there in the flesh, she was there in the sperit; an' I had n't no comfort in livin' when I see Jim so sot about her."

"Now ye kinder try me, Leeweeze, when ye go on so. I 've got a boy o' my own, an' I want him ter vally his mother. I sh'd tho't yer might-er respected Jim's feelin's."

"But I tell yer, Charlotte, it was like this with him, — not his *mother*, but *his* mother. I'd got ter give in ter thet old woman, not becos 't was my dooty, but becos 't was his will 't I should. Jim's ez domineerin' ez the next one; an' his pride teached him thet his mother was part 'n' passel of him, an' I'd oughter take her with him. Them was his feelin's, an' I did n't respect 'em, — no, not a mite. I uster get real bitter dwellin' on it, an' I'd say ter myself, ef it's sech a towerin' thing ter be this man's mother, why ain't it somethin' ter be his wife? Why don't I count for nothin' 't all with him? And I'd fret tell I was most wild; for nothin' took my mind off 'n it. I could fret jest ez well when I was doin' up my work, sweepin' from the north pole ter the south pole in thet shackly old house ez any other time. But the more I thought on it the more I was fo'ced ter own thet Jim was wayed like his mother. I could see her ways, some on 'em, right over again in him. I did n't wanter own it; but there 't was. An' then I'd think ter myself, ' Come, Louisa, why can't you get along with one o' those Flints ez well ez the other?' but I could n't make it the same noway; an' I kep' goin' over thet tex' where it says thet no one shell sarve two masters, fer he shell hate the one an' love the other; an' so 't was with me about them two. Likely 't was becos I was so wicked, wa'n't it?"

"No, child, I don't think 't was clear wicked-ness; 't was on'y natur'. Yer'm got to enjure yer husband's faults, an' thet's the burden thet fits ter yer shoulders; but I don't rightly see what clear call ye hev ter bear an' forbear with yer mother-in-law to the eend o' time. Yer did n't promise nor vow her nothin', did ye? No, she ain't no mastery over ye by rights; an' I say let her go ter her own folks ter find enjurin' patience.' T ain't in reason thet son's wife kin be own daughter ter nobody, let alone them thet's sech ez she is. We can't live our lives but onct, an' she can't be the fust tho't in no house no more. Thet's hard lines, I know; but it's what I've got ter realize when my time comes."

"Oh, Charlotte, yer're enough sight dif'rent from Mother Flint; nobody'd ever wish yer further; but I railly think Jim wanted her ter go ter keep house fer her brother, fer all he was so stiff with me about it. Yes, he's pretty much lost all the good opinion he ever hed o' me. He took ter sayin' things thet was real cruel; he could be the most sarcastic thet ever was. I come out in religion about the time I was goin' with Jim, an' I wanted he should too; but he wa'n't ready then, an' he don't belong now, an' I don't know 's he ever will. He's took up a real tauntin' way now about religion, always won-derin' why sech religious creturs ez women is can't live together ez peaceable ez ev'ry-day sinners does.   Yes, he 's ready 'nough to fling that at me, sence he 's so disappointed in me.   Well, it 's all over with us.   He knows my faults, an' I know his'n, an' ev'rythin 's ended an' done with."

" No, yer redic'lous child.   What air ye both on ye but a couple o' childun, settin' an' playin' scorn each ter t' other?   Yer lives is jest a beginnin' in airnest.   Fer pity's sake ! ye did n't expect ter walk through life a-steppin' on ter roses like two figgers on a valintine, did ye?   Yer ain't lived very long inter this here world, but I sh'd tho't yer 'd knowed better 'n thet.   No : now 's the time, when ye know each other's faults ter show thet ye ain't all faults.   The 's somethin' left yit ter count on.   Jim ain't quite a monster, by all 't I c'n make out ('t would n't be safe fer me ter say so anyhow), an' I know yer ain't nothin' but a poor little goose.   The 's a futur, an' one wuth havin', fer ye yit, or I ain't no prophet."

" Charlotte, I 'm 'fraid you don't know Jim ez well 's I do," replied the girl, sadly.   " He don't think o' me ez he did onct.   He thinks his mother 's old, an' hes seen trials, but thet I ain't no excuse for my bad tempers, an' he says, — but there, I won't tell what he says, — I 've told too much, a'ready."

" It 's my idee thet Master Jim 's a good deal

more ter blame in all this fuss than what yer
be, yer poor child," began Charlotte, with heat;
then, touched by the mute appeal of the worn
face, she concluded gently, " but it don't help
yer none ter dwell on thet, dooz it? "

"Oh, no, no, it ain't what he said ter me, it's
what I said an' done ter him that comes back
now ter trouble me most, an' keeps me so anxious in my mind. I b'lieve when we try to
please ourselves the most, givin' way t' our
feelin's, and talkin' back, we've got ter pay fer
it all afterwards."

"Yes, ef yer live long, yer'll feel thet more
an' more. Self-pleasin's a snare, whatever way
we sarch it out. It ain't no comfort ter look
back upon self-will, an' seekin' yer own pleasure. I 've hed my solemn times in my life,
when I was brung low with sickness an' trouble,
— when my baby was born, they all tho't I
couldn't never git up ag'in, — an' it all come
ter me then, clear ez day. Self-pleasin' was
dust an' ashes in my teeth, but ef I 'd ever giv'
a cup o' cold water ter my inemy, why, 't was
coolness ter my sperit."

The words of the faithful woman, who owed
nothing to the wisdom of books, but who had
patiently submitted to the discipline of life,
breathed such an influence as if her searching
questionings had been voiced in the poet's
language : —

"The pleasures thou hast planned,
  Where shall their memory be,
When the white angel with the freezing hand
  Shall sit and watch by thee?"

"Charlotte," whispered Louisa, after a silence, "I keep goin' an' goin' it over in my mind how I come off an' left him. I told him, after we'd hed one o' them talks, thet I couldn't stay there no longer, an' I'd leave him ter his mother, sence she was the one he thought the most on, an' I'd go home ter my own folks. And he said, never onct lookin' to-wards me, 'All right, please yerself; ther's nobody else kin please ye, thet's certin.' An' so I come off; but I shouldn't thought he'd took me ter my word so onfeelin'; an' only ter think, he wouldn't even look at me," repeated Louisa, dwelling piteously upon this crowning misery.

"Mebbe he dursn't look at ye, fer fear he'd break down," judiciously suggested Charlotte. "Yer take my word fer it, 't was thet. I guess I know a leetle more about the ways o' men-folks, an' about human natur' than what yer do, child." Charlotte caressed the slight hand that she had taken in her own with motherly tenderness.

"Yer hed a hard life on it, didn't ye?" questioned her young friend, momentarily diverted from her own interests.

"I made it hard fer myself." The words fell

slowly from her lips, and her strong, clear-cut profile was turned away from the listener. "Ev-'rybody in this town knows the story about me," she went on, in cold, measured tones; "how my husband was a drinking man, at times, though there wa'n't nothin' else ter bring ag'in him, an' a good-natur'd man when he was himself; but I was proud-sperited, and one time — I couldn't be'n in my right mind, no mor'n he was — I vexed him so with my tongue 't I driv' him away from home, an' he shipped fer a vy'ge, an' was lost with the schooner. Twenty year ago! twenty year ago!" she slowly repeated, looking fixedly into the dim vacancy of the room, as if she gazed far into the past.

"Don't, don't look like thet, Charlotte; don't take on!" called Louisa, "I'm sorry I spoke so. I never thought; why, I never see yer look like this" — catching hold of her gown with a childlike action, to which her friend presently responded, turning toward her again with her wonted aspect, "Don't go back to it all! I think yer're the best woman I ever see, an' always jest ez good an' sweet ez Cousin M'hal'! And ev'rybody says yer've brought up yer boy wonderful."

"Yes, I hed my boy," breathed the mother, with returning tranquillity.

"It fairly frightens me," cried Louisa, nervously renewing her troubled confessions, "ter find out how homesick I be here ter home. Ev'rything's so changed ter me, I feel ez ef I hed n't never lived here. I'm safter here from trouble, mebbe; but it's all so strange sence I come back seems so I can't stay;" and she moved restlessly from side to side.

"So yer find, after all, thet ez miz'able an' wretched ez you'n' Jim was together, you'm yit more miz'able an' wretched apart," Charlotte questioned, with a faint smile.   ·

"Oh, I dono's he wants ter lay eyes on me ag'in." (A pause.) "But, oh dear! I can't no more stay here than I could git inter the old chee-ry cradle in the garr't thet I was rocked in. I hed some bitter times, an' some hard cryin' spells over there; but — well, I *did* take more int'rest in things than I can now. Seems ez ef I was done with home fer good, an' I dono where I'll turn to now."

· "I'll tell ye, Leeweeze. Yer go home ter yer husban', yer know yer want ter; yer know well 'nough Jim'll jump over the house ter hev ye back ag'in, though yer pertend not; an' jest you try, now, an' see ef ye can't make of him. I ain't the one ter give ye no advice, but my life's giv' ye warnin', an' yer go ter yer own heart fer caounsel. Can't yer try ter rate yer husban' — an' other folks, too — 't won't do no hurt — 'cordin' to the best the' is in 'em, or even 'cordin' ter what they'm a-tryin' ter be,

more 'n what they actilly be, some on the time?
Thet's the kind o' marcy we all on us hes ter
cry fer.   Why, yer was speakin' jest now about
comin' out in religion; how do yer think the
good Lord kin count ye 'mong the number o'
his handmaids?   More by yer good desires in
yer prayers an' hymns than by yer righteous
sarvice, ain't it?   Oh! how kin we shet up our
hearts from folks lest the Lord should harden
his heart ag'inst us?"

"But Mother Flint?" demurred Louisa, repeating the dreaded name as if it had been that
of Mother Jezebel.

"Never yer mind about yer Mother Flint,"
responded her adviser, with decision.   "I'd do
the best I could, an' not trouble about old Mis'
Flint; an' yer see, now, ef it don't all come out
right at last."

Louisa scanned the speaker's kindly face, in
the endeavor to penetrate to the depths of this
oracular response.   The dimple in Charlotte's
cheek, — that one indestructible souvenir of
youth that continues to grace the human countenance through all the phases of maturity and
age — faintly played, combining with the humorous light that showed in her eyes to per-
plex the observer ;   and, after a prolonged
scrutiny, her young friend seemed to abandon
further research into the unfathomed wisdom
of the other's experience ;   but, sinking back

among her pillows, she announced, wearily, as if the confession were torn from her, —

" I suppose I shell hev ter go back," and, spent with the fatigues and emotions of the day, immediately burst into a passion of sobbing.

" Of course yer will, dear," briskly returned her companion with cheerful sympathy. " What else hev yer ben meanin' ter do, this whole enjurin' time ? "

Louisa neither denied nor affirmed this astute statement, but when Charlotte had finally soothed and quieted her, sent her to see if Aunt Eesther were not calling.

" No, child," announced Charlotte, on her return a few minutes later. " You 'm kinder weak and nervous, — thet's all; the' ain't nobody stirrin'."

" Well, I hear somebody now fast enough," insisted the invalid. " Hark ! "

" Well, true ez yer live the' is somebody now knockin' ter the front door.   I 'll go right away." And Charlotte hastened to answer the summons, which rapidly grew urgent.

Returning after a long absence, she found Louisa panting, flushed, and wide-eyed.   No need to tell her who the late visitor was.

" Leeweeze, I 'm afeerd ye don't know Jim Flint ez well ez I do," began Charlotte, in stern mimicry of her patient's recent words ; and then both women laughed and kissed and cried with a kind of soft violence quite unbefitting the dis-

12

cipline of the sickroom and the habits of rustic
impassibility.

"Yer see, Leeweeze,. yer ain't hed the hard
times all t' yerself. Yer husban's hed time ter
think over these things, too, an' he 's tho't ter some
puppus. I guess 't 'll be a long lesson ter both
on ye. But he never knowed a breath about yer
bein' sick these two three days tell one o' the
gang told him ter-night arter hours; an' then he
could n't git no team away up there ter the Dugway, so he travelled afoot ev'ry step, an' when I
let him in he was white 's a sheet, an' looked fit
ter drop. 'How 's my wife?' said he. 'Yer
wife 's a sufferin' woman,' said I; 'but her main
distress is in her mind.' And then, Leeweeze,
thet gret, terrible, sarcastic man you was a-tellin'
me on jest broke down an' cried like a baby, —
or a man; for they kin both on 'em cry with all
their might when they onct git fa'rly under way.
Matchment take ye both fer two o' the foolishest
young folks 't ever I see. I sha'n't do nothin'
more fer ye!"

After this style of rustic raillery tempered
with affection, the elder woman went on until
she had completed that minute account of the
interview which was eagerly exacted of her by
the patient.

"But then he started up, an' I tho't he would
ha' breshed me away from the door like a fly;
but I hild to, an' told him, 'No; you can't see

her ter-night. She's dreadful weak, an' nervious, an' I can't hev her gettin' all worked up; an', besides, yer don't want ter come in so, all unbeknownst ter her folks. Her ma's comin' home ter-morrer; she's ben sent fer, an' you come then.' I teched his pride pooty clus' with thet, so 't he giv' in; but he'll be here ter-morrer, an' then he wants ter be frien's with yer ma, an' all yer folks. And don't yer fret no more about poor old Mis' Flint; she's goin' ter keep house fer her brother. Did n't I tell ye 't would all come out right? I expect 't was more 'n hinted to her afore; but anyway Jim stopped a few minutes ter home on his way here, an' settled it. But yer oughter rej'ice with tremblin' over sech ez thet; an' I 'm sorry fer Mis' Flint; fer she's a mother, with a mother's feelin's, I know, even ef she don't make no very agreeable showin' on 'em. Mebbe yer'll come ter some better onderstandin' with her some day, spacially ef she lives to a good distance off."

"Oh, Charlotte, you do make me feel ashamed; but I can't seem to realize my wrong doin's the way I hed oughter. Seems though anybody would be solemnized ter fare so much better than they desarved; but I can't feel nothin' truly but glad, glad, glad!

"But I've got ter own up somethin';" resumed the patient after a pause, and with rather an abashed look. "What do yer think! — when I sent yer out ter listen ef Aunt Eesther wa'n't callin' I got thet pitcher o' water she brought up ter keep fer her straw-braidin', an' I drinked all the' was left in it!"

"The Lord preserve us!" ejaculated the watcher in consternation. "Well, well, an' I never see what you was at! What a han' yer be ter git roun' folks! I don't wonder Jim an' me don' stand no chance with ye. I hope an' pray ye won't hev ter suffer fer bein' so heedless an' keerless. Here now, time's come round agin ter give ye some more o' them powders."

But when the draft was prepared, and Charlotte had approached the bed, the deep breathing of its occupant told the nurse that the sudden slumber of physical exhaustion and mental relief had at last overpowered the irritated nerves of her restless charge.

"I declare, I won't wake her, not ter give her no doctor's stuff thet ever was pestled in a mortar!" rebelliously uttered Charlotte in subdued tones, but animated by a sense of reckless defiance that kept her intensely wakeful for the next hour, during which she anxiously watched over the sleeper.

"She seems ter rest jest ez peaceful ez though thet drink o' water hed n't harmed her one mite," finally murmured the watcher, relaxing her vigilance, and beginning to notice the chill of the night air as she shivered and drew up her shawl.

The night wore on, and still there was no change in the hushed repose that wrapped the house in silence. Charlotte at last rested her head for a moment, as she intended, on the light-stand beside the bed, and was presently fast asleep. The wan hours of morning stole through the room, the solemn glories of dawn marshalled in the heavens, and the cheerful light of a new day dwelt tenderly upon the soft innocence that informed the childlike face of one sleeper and threw a ray of consecration upon the worn features of the other, that now showed some traces of youthful grace, as touched by the soothing spell of slumber. And the place was sacred to the visible presence of that influence which we name the ever-womanly, — that influence which, albeit with many errors, and amid occasional reproach, still safely guards and cherishes the one great trust of humanity, still is true to the duties, the hopes, and the affections that centre in the home.

"GOOD-BY, good-by, Mrs. Dawley. I ought to have been off with the others, instead of outstaying the season, like a belated blue-bottle. You must be glad to see the last of us, for we have been the hungriest hunters that ever tramped the Flats, and we've made you no end of cooking. You and Dawley can settle down to a quiet life now. You'll be snug and comfortable enough here next week, at Thanks-giving, won't you?"

The young woman to whom this effusively cheerful leave-taking was addressed, while her hand was held a second longer than the speaker had intended before meeting the dumb appeal of her questioning eyes, made no very relevant or expansive answer, being, indeed, little used to deal in other than the most practical expressions of personal interest.

"It's comin' on ter rain," she announced, in her usual languid and plaintive monotone. "Block Island looms up, and the clouds looks oily. Yer better take the umbrel', Mr. Crown-inshield, or yer'll ketch yer death. Hitty, run an' fetch it, Quick! yer father's waitin' out. there."

Mr. Crowninshield considerately restrained the movement of impatience with which he would have declined the anxiously proffered attention, but took refuge from the unconscious revelation of nameless distress written on Susan Dawley's unschooled features in a final romp with the children; and, with an exchange of shouted good-byes between him and them, and the last courtesies of taking leave of their mother, he was driven away to the station by Dawley, in whose house a few autumn visitors had been boarding while their host accompanied them in their daily hunting-tramps.

Susan stood on the rough door-stone of the old Dawley homestead, transfixed, as it seemed, in the stillness of patient pain, and looking after the two figures as they disappeared around the turn in the road, — one so firm, easy, and self-reliant in its air, the other obscurely hinting a sullen defiance in the ignoble lines of its brute strength, and suggesting the saying in which Le Roux has acutely expressed the bucolic quality, "The peasant is a man only as a block of marble is a statue."

She was still mechanically looking into the distance with eyes that saw nothing, when her eldest girl pulled her gown to make her hear her reiteration of "Marmer, baby's all waked up,

.and she 's fixin' ter cry!" The mother took the
fretful, ailing child, and tried to hush its weakly,
wretched wailings. But while she monotonously
soothed and crooned, her consciousness was
filled with other thoughts than such as were concerned with the helpless creature so seldom out
of her arms.

This woman of twenty-six had borne seven
children, and had cried herself heartsick and
despairing over the graves of three of them, as
they were made in the bleak spot on the wind-
swept hill where the dead and gone Dawleys of
a hundred years lay in their unmarked, un-
guarded mounds, and slept that satisfactory
slumber which wraps the virtuous yeomanry
who are buried in their own acres; albeit their
repose was but little respected by the heavy-
treading cattle, or the curiously browsing sheep.

Not that Susan dwelt bitterly upon these mortuary humiliations. She had known no other
conditions on the adjoining farm, her meagre
patrimony, where she had lived until her marriage at sixteen; and the usages of these two
places comprised nearly all that she knew of the
world. She had never penetrated the limits of
her township, and of its villages she had never
seen the chief. Never had she shared in the
bustle and the gayeties of the Carcassonne of her
province, never yet had realized her childish
hopes of joining in its Fourth-of-July pageants,

or of beholding that palpable dream of all infantile delights, the toy-shop window, crowded with dolls that were seated in a row, each bearing her price-ticket in her lap, as if the display were a crude tableau of a sale of Circassian beauties. When she was first married her husband used to talk of taking her there when he marketed his farm products, and even now he would sometimes say, "I tell you, Suse, some day, when it's good goin', an' you ain't no butter to make, an' the childun ain't sick, an' I have n't no newspaper ter read, nor nothin' ter hender, I'd jest ez lives ez not take ye over ter the 'ville ter do yer tradin'." But such complacent offers came less and less frequently, and Susan's timidity, indifference, tact, or possibly some more complex feeling than these, saved her from the error of taking this marital magnanimity too literally.

She had never conquered that oppressive timidity with which she had always regarded Jackson Dawley, though they had spent the greater part of their lives together. She used to suffer with a mute dread of the rough boy, just as she shrank from his great dogs; and once she saw him beating his horse in a rage that sent her cowering away, with the feeling (for she was then dimly aware of the shape her future was to take), that it would be a pitiable thing to be wife to a man capable of such savagery.

They had not been schoolmates, for Susan's delicate constitution, the distance from the schoolhouse, and her grandmother's indulgence to an orphan, had nearly deprived her of the educational opportunities afforded by her native district. "What kinder diff'unce did it make?" demanded her grandfather, with virile disgust; for, though he was a yeoman of few acres, he was none the less imbued with the fine old feudal spirit of the Rhode Island landholder, and sorely deplored the lack of heirs male "to bear up the Mowry name." He deprecated the folly of keeping his granddaughter. at school after her fourteenth year. "She's nothin' but a no-account little dish-washer, anyway, and she c'n larn *her* business best 'round house, 'cordin' ter my notion." In the routine of farmhouse work Susan grew to be an awkward, old-fashioned girl, speaking the quaint dialect of her grandparents in archaic purity, free from the coarse alloy of modern slang. Dame Diffidence, of Doubting Castle, herself, was not more shy than Susan; and the solitary life of the farm had made her odd and indescribably rustic, but she was untouched by the rough influences of the sordid village life as it is cheapened by the rude publicity of the street and the shop. When she went out "to walk abroad," as she phrased it, she buried her features in a sunbonnet as deep as the Quaker head-covering, and thus equipped

with modesty's shield and defence, remotely
wondered at the hardihood of the girls whom
she saw growing bold in unyouthful defiance as
they flaunted their imitation fineries in the garish
gaze of that school of cynicism, the sidewalk.
All her associations were clean and pure — free
from the taint of a selfish and dangerous vanity.
The year in its round kept her among healthful
rustic sights and sounds, and brought her the
wholesome companionship of dumb life, in the
cade lambs and belated chickens, for whom she
knit stockings, as her grandmother had it, and
whom she at least established in the warmest
corner of the kitchen, whence mysterious cluck-
ings and peepings issued from a dilapidated basket.   Through all the season's changes of that
country life, which has its idyllic aspects to an
observer, but is full of the prose of the severest
toil, she was zealous and diligent, from the first
pulling of spring greens in the brook-meadow
to the soap-making in the fall, when a bent, old,
black witch stirred the gypsy caldron hung under the great apple-tree, and Susan helped her
grandmother to accomplish those labors and
observe those traditionary customs prescribed
by rustic superstition, lest, if they were neglected, the much-placated soap should refuse
"to come."

Her fifteenth summer brought her that pre-
mature inheritance of beauty and bloom that

is early won and early lost; and its exquisite dazzle
brought an answering gleam to the dullest eyes.
The gruff old Irishman who had for years helped
on the farm in haying-time, but with whom Susan
had never felt well acquainted, owing to his
sedulously cultivated deafness, and his confusing
habit of invariably shouting "Mim!" in perfunc-
tory reply to all feminine interrogations, — even
he now doubled her embarrassment by deliber-
ately surveying her, and emerging from his inarticulate state with the emphatic declaration that
she was the makings of a fine girl; further indulging in a warm comparison between her and
one "Miss Honora McGlathery, who was the
beautifullest lady, and lived in a grand house,
just forninst the Phaynix Park," with some further
particulars respecting that semi-mythical personage, of whose name, indeed, old Phelim's cronies
often had occasion to be weary. And the cheery
little English woman, a red-cloaked, courtesying
old-world figure, that sometimes, in a press of
work, brought an oddly foreign presence into
the Mowry surroundings, smilingly announced,
"She 've grown to be the handsome gell, ma'am;
she 's as slim as slim; her eyes are as black as
black; her skin is white as milk; her hair is
that fair and curly; and she has the feeturs of
a lady born, has Susan Mowry;" and as the
language of this eulogy very nearly resembles
that of the descriptions of young country maids

in fairy tales, it may well serve to render the values of an unspoiled, primitive beauty.

It was not at all in consequence of Susan's bloom, which inspired these international compliments, but because of her grandmother's death and her grandfather's decline, that her fate was now to be decided, and her inheritance to pass into the keeping of Jackson Dawley. Surely this was an idyllic marriage! What more charming pastoral could there be than the tender union of two simple young lives? But Susan shrank with unfeigned distaste from the arrangement, actually throwing her apron over her head and running away when she saw her destined swain doubtfully approaching, by which blindly impulsive retreat she not only got an ignominious fall, but incurred the weight of her grandfather's sarcasms. Jackson's only responses to the paternal urgings were reluctantly given, but were of a character that slightly discouraged the elder Dawley in his first keen insistance upon the scheme. "Tell you how 't is, neighbor," frankly announced Old Man Dawley (to give him the derisive title that his hypochondriac notions had gained for him in his middle-age), "tell you jest what," he pursued, in the vigorous but enigmatic idiom which conveys the mortification of disappointed match-makers, "them sticks won't fight."

"And I tell you they shell!" explosively re-

torted Granther Mowry, with a fine contempt for
the cobweb scruples of his crony, and bringing
down his ponderous fist with an emphasis that
shook a stone or two from the tottering boundary-
wall between the farms.   "Say" (with an irritated disgust at the other's faint-heartedness),
"what ails ye, anyhow?   D'ye think I don't
know my own mind?"

Susan's mind in the matter, had it been sought,
could not have been very definitely stated.   She
was but dimly conscious of the wrong done to
her youth by the fate which she was forced to
accept at the sordid hands of her arbitrary elders.
That Jackson Dawley was a less ideal figure than
even the conventional youths of those stories of
not too refined a tone that she was at much pains
to spell out of the village paper, might perhaps
be accounted but a flimsy objection.

Who was there to teach her that a loveless
marriage was an unholy one?   From whom
could she have learned that the vows of marriage were in no degree less solemn and sacred
than the ceremonies of the Christian sacraments?
Her own heart might intuitively prompt her to
these beliefs; but who was to credit them with
the stamp of experience and authority?   Would
it be her grandmother, tottering into her second
childhood just as Susan's young feet began to
tread the perplexed path of life?   Or would it
be the spinster schoolmistress who sometimes

boarded at the Mowry house on her rounds? —
a desiccated personality; a being of superlative
refinement, who never spoke of a baby but
under the withering ·title of "a babe," who
would not refer to a housebreaker in less polite
language than to inquire "what sort of a looking
gentleman did he appear to be?" and who, in
preparing fruit for the table, never "snuffed"
the strawberries as her honest grandmother
did, nor "hulled them," as her mother had
it, but with accurate elegance, "removed the
calyxes." From a schooling in this learned
lady's somewhat academic conceptions of life
how much of saving wisdom would our poor
Susan learn?

Or was it from the literature or other influences of the intermittent Sunday-school at which
she was an infrequent attendant that she could
get any guidance in these questions? The books
were dumb, and gave no sign; anything having
the most remote bearing on the one vital question which the young and ignorant readers would
be called on to decide being excluded with feverish care from their negative pages. And the
teachers, in all their associations with the young
girls of their classes, never strengthened their
work by that community of interests which
might have been formed between the elders and
the juniors if motherly wisdom or sisterly sympathy had not stopped just short of the one

point of central importance in the future of these immature lives.

Nor had Jackson, when bidden by his father, in Susan's behalf, to look on her, and love, as in duty bound, any other excuse for his unwillingness to obey than his questionable interest in "that Lewis girl," as she was conspicuously known in the mill where she worked, and in the sidewalk parlance of the 'ville. That Jackson had long been the admirer-in-chief of this not inexorable young person, his father well knew, and was exceedingly anxious to sever the connection, not only from the fine-spun motives of moral prudence, but for the good and sufficient reason that the Lewis girl had nothing but the clothes she stood in, and Susan was a "gal o' prop'ty," with fifty acres of land coming to her, and hundreds of dollars in the savings bank besides. The mundane old rustic put aside all scruples concerning the undesirable Miss Lewis with a readiness that was nothing less than Chesterfieldian. "Jinny Lewis never wa'n't none too good," was his cynical conclusion; and "That's *her* lookout," was the dry rejoinder to the query as to what would become of her, which Jackson, with no unmanly spirit, addressed to his honored parent. ·

So the marriage of reason, which occurs not only in the great world, but is also evolved under those sordid conditions of bucolic life which

foster the mercenary spirit, was accomplished;
and it had brought its penalty in the weight of
the ten years that had rested heavily on the
slight shoulders of the weaker party to the con-
tract. These weary years had visited Susan
with ill health that had sadly obscured her
beauty. The pure and delicate contours of
feature still asserted their lasting perfection;
but all the freshness and light had faded out of
the face; its bloom had gone; the lids showed
a spiritless droop; and some deeper dejection
than such as is bred of the dulness of a drudging routine gave a rude pathos to the Yankee
accent that lent its prolonged melancholy to her
tones. Indeed, Mr. Crowninshield's only departure from that grave and punctilious respect
which his hostess, present or absent, received
from him, was made in that allusion to this
characteristic utterance which was conveyed in
his remark to a fellow-sportsman that Dawley's
wife ought to be called Mrs. *Drawley*.

Susan Dawley could have but little pride or
pleasure in her children. They were all, like
the fretful, restless infant whom she now hushed
and rocked, predestined to be blights, not blos-
soms, on the hardy old stock which had suddenly withered, after a century's seasoning,
under the adverse conditions to which these
pale and spiritless little folks succumbed. The
cruel, penetrating dampness of the mists from

Cedar Pond, which the old house greedily drank
in at its gaping crannies, and the deathly chill
from the side-hill against which it was built, so
that light and air were shut out from one of its
four walls, drained away the feeble vitality with
which they began that struggle for breath which
we hail as life.   It was but a sorry Eden — that
home in which Susan, on her first coming to it,
had been met on the threshold of her room by
the portent of a cold, coiling black snake — no
such infrequent guest, as she had learned by a
longer experience of the persistent dampness
and darkness of a house partly entombed in the
hillside.

Of course she had heard something and had
divined more of that wretched story of Jinny
Lewis; and though the girl, after her dismissal
from the factory, had left the 'ville to look for
work in Providence, as she said, Susan still per-
turbedly associated her bold, hardened, unyouthful beauty with her late dwelling-place, and
never ceased to feel an unreasoning jealousy at
her husband's errands there, and an instinctive
shrinking from the sight of a town that, to the
severity of her conception, lay under the shadow
of a great guilt.   She thought of this village, to
her so inextricably connected with the wrongs
of a shameful history, with some touch of that
ascetic spirit which she drew from the Quaker
great-grandsire of whom she had often heard it

told how when he was aboard ship, a-sailing on
the high seas, and the captain put into London
town, he would not so much as look upon Baby-
lon, but bore his testimony against her iniquities
by staying below reading the Word until the
day came to weigh anchor; and, when urged to
go ashore, saying only, " Friend, thou art an
unstable counsellor; " or ejaculating, " Lord,
turn Thou away mine eyes from beholding
vanity."

Jackson neither comprehended nor was interested in his wife's individuality. Her moods, as
far as he noted them, were such as to provoke
his impatience or kindle his resentment. Nor
could he ever quite forgive her former owner-
ship of the acres she had meekly brought
him. His most tolerant estimate of her was
that of a mild contempt; his utmost good-nature
toward her but faintly suggested the strength
of the ties that bound him to his children; for
he was an indulgent father. He suffered in the
deaths of the children with a fierce and angry
passion of loss, not unmingled with the spirit of
reproach. If Susan had known scarlet fever
when she saw it, their eldest girl might have
lived, and her death was as a rankling wrong in
the breast of her father. " I 'd ruther ha' lost
the best cow in my yard," he told Mr. Crowninshield, with the unconscious sincerity of a hard
man measuring his sorest regrets by the only

standard of values within the grasp of his nature.
But the children, timid and shrinking, like their
mother, and in some occult way dimly aware of
the invisible barrier that separated the nearer
parent from the solicitous one, often met his affection with a peevish coldness for which he secretly
blamed Susan, and perhaps with reason; for, if
the average wife and mother is sometimes capable of an unworthy jealousy over the affections
of her children, and yields their father a share
in them only as a dole, can an unloved and un-
loving woman be expected to show any finer
sense of the mutual magnanimity of the domestic relations? Nature reserves this certain re-
source, albeit an ungenerous one, to the most
unhappy woman, that her children's hearts are
in her hand, and she may turn them whitherso-
ever she will. Her little child is her inalienable
possession, and whoever shares its love with her
must often accept as a grace that which might
be claimed as a right.

Susan, either intent on her ailing child or
wrapped in her unwelcome thoughts, did not
notice that the other children had slipped away
into the bedroom; did not heed the shaggy Irish
setter who, after a gloomy meditation upon his
master's mortifying desertion of him, finally approached his mistress, of whom he commonly
made but small account, to lay his head in her
lap, for the sake of society, and with a view to

breakfast, vigorously expressed in the thumpings
of an energetic tail; nor did she see the coarse
black net cap of her mother-in-law, as its active
wearer whisked by the kitchen window a second
before her appearance in the room.

"My pity! Suse Dawley! 't fa'ly makes me
ache ter see yer a-settin' there wastin' daylight
hummin' ter that ar child like a bee in a bottle,
an' all o' them young uns o' yourn highted inter
the best bedroom, — gone there ter riot and
carouse, I 'll lay a penny."

But this scathing description was much more
forcible than the reality of their feeble play at
the illness which was so often a serious experience with them; for they had all crept into bed,
the better to play at being sick and sending for
the doctor. Dame Dawley dashed in upon them,
and Susan passively listened to the confused
sounds of admonition, discipline, and chastise-
ment, mingled with an ebullition of childish tears
and wrath. The grandmother presently stood
in the doorway, reddened and rumpled, but vic-
torious. The spark of righteous anger kindled
in her eye, but further facial expression was inevitably limited by the curiously intricate fret-
work of wrinkles which masked the good lady's
features. If soul had ever sat enthroned in her
countenance, it had now for many years been
meanly imprisoned within this enclosure, and
could seldom be seen to peep through the bars.

" Here they was," she shouted, more in anger
than in sorrow, "sure 'nough, a twistin' an' a
turnin', an' a wearin' out o' good sheets, wuth
'nough sight more 'n their necks be. Yer Ben
Franklin, look here now! What ye done ter old
Dobbin? Whiar's he gone ter? Yer gran'-
father says ye must ha' lef' the bars down so 't
he got outer the lot."

" I never done no sech a thing. I tell ye I
ain't seen hide nor hair on him!" clamorously
asserted the puny philosopher of the house of
Dawley, with exhaustive literalness of diction.

His assailant turned upon the next victim, —

" Wal, Susan, thiar yer be yit! An' tendin'
baby 's full ez lazy work fer a woman ez fishin'
is fer the men-folks."

Susan indulged in the retort feminine, —

" Mebbe it' s so long sence yer done that
kinder work yer 'm furgot how it draws onto
the shoulders, an' makes yer side ache an' smart
every time ye draw breath."

" Not thet sorter heft would n't," returned
the grandam, nowise disconcerted, and with a
meaning sneer at the puny proportions of her
infantile descendant. " When *I* hed babies I
hed babies; they wa'n't rag dawls, they wa'n't."
With this historical statement, Mrs. Dawley
emitted a short laugh, of the most trenchant
quality.

Susan, who was no match for her venerable

relative in these personal sallies, instinctively clasped her maligned infant closer to her breast, as she drew her breath hard and flushed deep with maternal rage, but sat speechless and staring while the shaft quivered in her wound.

"Wal," resumed the old dame, in a more pacific tone, as though magnanimously satisfied with her two righteous victories over her guilty juniors, "s'pose I must skite hum now an' hist on the dinner-pot. I'm agreeable for havin' dinner an' supper together these here short days, but Dawley he can't never git enough. When the Lord created man he gin him a ter'ble appetite fer vittles," she mused, with the grimness of a life-long observer of that phenomenon.

"How *is* Father Dawley?" asked Susan, forcing herself to meet these friendly overtures.

"The Lord knows, I don't," piously responded his spouse. "His complaints comes an' goes, like the old woman's soap. He's had the hypo' now forty year runnin', an' I believe it's healthy. Sometimes I think he's wus sence he gin up the farm ter Jackson, an' then agin I dono. Ef he scratches his finger he's same's down with the lockjaw; an' ef he gits a twinge o' toothache he's goin' ter hev the tickdullroo, sure. The schoolmaster down to Number Six, he's another one; 's got ez many aches an' pains ez there be pins an' needles in a cushin. I wouldn't give much fer his schoolin', but ter

be sure, he keeps *hours* enough.   Wal, he comes
over nights ter see the old man 'n' cuddunk with
him, 'n' they set 'n' drink hot peppermint 'n'
sage tea, 'n' tell over their poor spells.   Dawley's main fret jest now is 'bout his fun'l.   He 's
dreadful feared I won't do well by him.   ' Old
man,' says I, ' don't yer worry.   I 'll see yer
through when 't comes ter that.   D' yer s'pose
I sh'd take any satisfaction 't all in it, ef things
was skinched up,' says I.   ' Deary me,' says he,
an' he fetched a groan with ev'ry breath he
drawed, ' I sha'n't live this night out.   I sha'n't
never see ter-morrer mornin'.'   'Wal,' says I, 'ef
yer don't, I c'n fly roun' an' git things enough
fer the fun'l, ef forty folks stays ter dinner.
We 'm jest killed,' says I, ' an' spare-ribs an' pork-
turkeys relishes fust rate to a fun'l dinner,' says
I.   He kinder sperrited up at that, an' told that
old story about his Cousin Congdon, how she
alwas kep' a ham in the house in case Congdon
should die, an' how Congdon et it to her fun'l
arter all.   But land!   I must go right off now,
it begins ter sprenkle.   I knowed 't would rain,
fer Block Island light streamed acrost las' night.
Say, Susan, gimme some o' them little aprons
ter make, I c'n do 'em well 's not; " and the active old woman dived into a heap of coarse sew-
ing that piled the work-basket.   " My glory, I
guess I c'n do that one with my old eyes ez
well ez you 'm begun it; looker them great big

stitches grinnin' at yer all acrost it!   Sartinly,
Susan " (with a sudden diversion to the baby),
"that child is gonter look dreadfully like Old
Man, sartin she is," indicating by an expressive
grimace, the grotesque likeness between the
drawn and puckered features, just quivering in
a cry, and the aged and tremulous countenance
of the venerable invalid.   "Wal, what can't be
cured must be endoored.   Metty take alivins,
'ittle sissy!   Shake a day-day ter gra'ma, hey?
Wal, good-by, Susan; take good keer on yerself now — ez ye seem likely ter!"   With this
parting shot the old lady took her departure,
leaving Susan somewhat less perturbed in spirit
than her visitor could have desired.

Susan's thoughts had not yet returned from
their melancholy wanderings to the worn channels of domestic routine, and she still kept her
place, while her morning's work awaited her
at the uncleared table.   The American breakfast flourished in all its pristine luxuriance
in the house of Jackson Dawley, and Susan,
who was a good cook, though her neighbors
declared her to be a slack housekeeper, had
never yet found that the most fastidious of any
hunting party failed to welcome her savory
dishes, let them appear when they might.   She
had never cared to adapt her service to the
tastes of any of her guests, until, with a dim consciousness that all was not just as Mr. Crownin-

shield would wish, she began to set her dinner-
table in the centre of the room, instead of leaving it against the wall, and to disturb the ancient
solitary reign of the dust and cobwebs that had
gathered in the old house as its mistress lost
more and more of her girlish zeal for housewifery.   But lately she had attacked these dominant foes with a vigor that had left more signs
of rugged toil on the shapely hand and arm
than had marred them since, as was said of her,
she began to lose all her ambition.

It was a strange fate that she, who had never
before taken note of her autumn guests, to
whom she might frankly have said, " Come as
shadows, so depart," should have conceived this
forlornly stifled regard, this piteously grotesque
hero-worship for one who had always treated
her with a scrupulously distant respect, in which
there was no hint of any constraint that might
suggest a veiled interest in a woman whose
hopeless secret could not be guarded from him.
Not unwilling to peruse the lovely lines of her
pure and pensive profile, whenever he happened
to note that it was near, — which was not so often
as might possibly have been the case if he had
not had an absorbing subject of reverie wherewith to fill the few intervals of leisure from the
excitement of sport, — he was always quick to
avert his glance when he saw the shy distress,
and, of late, the deeper pain of consciousness,

caused by his notice. It was one of the few intense feelings she had ever known, though of so different an order from that with which she had repelled the too free admiration of a former guest, protecting herself by the presence of her children. Now she secretly worshipped a man of no very remarkable mould, idealizing him for the generous heights to which his nature rose, in her simple apprehension, because, because— oh, how poor a tale has love to tell of the why and wherefore of its unquestioning devotion! If this stranger spoke in a different tone, treated her with another manner, and looked at her with kinder eyes than she had ever known, what spell could thus be wrought to move any but the weakest heart from the fast moorings of duty? And kindness was not wholly a new thing to Susan. She had had much kindness from — her grandmother! If in those girlish days she had dreamed of a future that life had never brought her, did she not assure herself, in her matronhood, that she could never think of any less unselfish love than the love of her poor, suffering children, who needed her so much? What right had she to indulge in gratitude to a stranger for the consideration which he habitually showed to women, and which was now deepened by an influence of which, it is true, she knew nothing? Because a man who flings his torn coat at his wife as she is walk-

ing the room holding her restless child, with a
muttered order to mend it straightway, which
sounds more like an enemy's curse than a household blessing, contrasts unfavorably with another
who asks a similar service with gentleness, ac-
cepts it with friendliness, and acknowledges it
by some kindly attention to the children, it was
none the less a sign of innate morbidness in
Susan that she dwelt upon these differences
with a bitterness that threatened the obliga-
tions of honor, truth, and loyalty. Poor soul!
she was born with that unhappy tendency
which, though she could not have named it,
was none the less real in its cravings, — the
spirit of romance. If a woman's innocent turn
for the romantic is quite denied its natural means
of expression, — if there is no conveniently
neutral lay-figure at hand which she may law-
fully embellish with the drapery of her idealisms,
as she lately dressed her passive doll, — then
expect a grotesque or a tragical perversion of
these thwarted instincts. Said they not well,
our pastors and masters, when they told us in
our simple youth that romance was a dangerous thing? Susan had escaped some obvious
dangers to the purity and delicacy of her womanhood in dwelling apart from the coarse village life ; but solitude also has its peculiar
snares, its tendencies to egotism and morbid
introspection ; and perhaps the bustle of a

street, or the gossip of elbowing neighbors, though not the finest of influences, might have been wholesome for this brooding spirit, and might have dulled its pain. Susan was not altogether in fault that there was so great a lack of harmony between her nature and its environments that her affections inevitably clung to the best representative of that worthier phase of life to which, among all her untoward surroundings, she unconsciously aspired. Bred in so dense an atmosphere of rusticity that social ambitions, in the ordinary sense, were utterly wanting to her experience, her spontaneous recognition of any substantial superiority of nurture was singularly quick and genuine. Many of us are born out of the nests where we belong, —young eagles are brooded by doves, and birds of paradise come into plumage beneath the wings of crows and vultures. Only, if the nestling never sings such notes as might have been its own in its proper home, and so never finds its true mate, why, that is but another of the many cruel tales of step-dame Nature's ungentle rule.

" Look at the wasted seeds that autumn scatters,
  The myriad germs that Nature shapes and shatters."

Susan had not glided into the habit of letting her thoughts dwell upon one of whom she had no right to think, and who, as the sure instinct

of hopeless love instructed her, thought not of
her at all, without some natural pangs of humiliation, some scourgings of self-reproach.   Between
fancy and fact, between principle and folly, she
traversed many tortuous paths of reverie.   " He
never even wanted ter say anything he should n't
ha' said," she used to tell her conscience defiantly,
so that that grim monitor might be hushed;
while in deeper murmurings than those of vanity
she told herself, as a smile of childish pleasure
lighted her faded beauty, "Seems as if he alwas
liked ter see me wear my blue gownd.   I heerd
him tell Hitty, ' Yer mother looks like Mony
Lizy ter-day.'   I dono who she was; but I don't
believe she was the one that giv' him the book."
Poor Susan had not been long in perceiving the
care with which, for some inscrutable reason,
Mr. Crowninshield kept a certain book among
the few that he brought with him, and that lay
about his room.   She studied it with jealous
passion, divining, heaven knows by what occult
sense, that it was from a woman, though the
mysterious initials M. D. L., over which she
pored until she gave them positive individuality,
were in the large, free, Minerva hand to which
at that day feminine chirographers seldom aspired.   The contents told her nothing, sedulously
as she scanned them; for it was a volume men-
tally described by her as one of " poems and
poetry, and such," and of course not to be

understood by anybody. But her resentment
toward it was as vivid as if it had been a sentient
thing. In one of her curiously childish passions
of wrathful jealousy she flung the offending book
as far as her utmost strength could send it, then
caught it up in a pallid fright, trembling lest
it should have been so marked as to arouse
the displeasure of its owner. If the poor girl's
mad demeanor was such as would better suit
with the favorite of a harem than with the mistress of a civilized home, it must be owned that
there had been no such efficient leaven of Christianity in Susan's nurture as to differentiate her
very widely from that unknown Indian woman
who might have had her wigwam dwelling on the
same sheltered spot beside the lake where
Susan's hearth-fire now burned. Weak and
childish still, though the mother of children;
never having been led by a strong and tender
hand; knowing religion only as a fluctuating
emotion, and not as a moving principle of life;
isolated from that social influence and opinion
which to her was but a distant shadow, — she
had very nearly lost sight of those traditions the
influence of which should have checked the
tumult of her impulses.

But now, as her thoughts dwelt painfully upon
these things, while her hands were busied with
her household duties, her pale cheeks suddenly
glowed with an honest blush as the keen dart

of shame pierced the idlesse of her unworthy dreamings. In the searching light of her contrite questionings what was she? what had she half descended to be in thought? " Oh, my soul ! " she groaned, "what be I better 'n Jinny Lewis ? " She shuddered in the strong revulsion of feeling that laid bare the ignoble reality of her long self-deception, and her trembling hands almost refused to do their offices. The children saw her agitation, and gathered about her, thinking that she shared their fear of the great darkness with which the sou'wester, now bursting in gusty fury upon them, filled the house, as if with a sinister presence. The sky lowered angrily dark, as in a summer tempest, then faintly lightened, as the rushing whiteness of the rain slanted solidly down, enclosing the lonely homestead in a watery sphere, which receded as the darkness shut down again, and the clouds girded up their strength for another savage onset.

In the momentary lull of roaring waters and tossing branches, an importunate knocking at the outer door at length made itself heard, and Susan, without a thought of hesitation, opened it to admit the very spirit of the storm, if so potent an essence had indeed condescended to appear in the person of a bent and withered little old man, opaquely black of visage, very much rent and torn as to his wind-tossed garments, that streamed with rain in every rag and

tatter, and very abject in his forlorn and shivering aspect.   His reception from the house-mis-
tress was as cordial as it would naturally be made
by one who saw in the half-barbaric figure of
old Quacca Noca no hideous portent, but merely
a familiar personality, to be greeted with the
urgency of rustic hospitality.

"Why, Quacca! why did n't ye come right in
outer the wet?   Come ter the fire, do.   Set right
down in the big cheer, and I 'll fetch ye a dish
o' tea."

"'Fore the Lord, mistis," piously ejaculated
the chattering old negro, with a simian gesturing
and show of teeth, "I see lightnin' jes' then, —
reg'lar jig-jag lightnin'!   But I 'specs 't won't
harm folks none; it's got all the heat warped
out on it this time o' the year.   Yes, mistis;
thenk *you*, mistis," — with a low, deprecatory
chuckle, as the dish of tea, with sundry more
substantial dishes, was set before him; "much
obleeged to you.   Yes, mistis, yer Aunt Dimmis she's 'bout the same.   The nat'ral bone-
setter says 't her back's got sprung over ter one
side, an' he dono 's he kin pry it round agin;
he 'specs now she 'll be a poor old hypocrite ter
the end of her days.   Yes, mistis, yes, I 'specs
she will," he nodded, in cheerful conclusion, with
the same supple and insinuating air that graced
the utterance of his frequent "thenk you."
Quacca's manners had been formed in the school

14

of slavery; for his grandfather had been shipped
from Guinea, and his father, born a slave, had
received as a part of his " freedom suit " his
" freedom stockings," knitted at generous length
by the industrious hands of his young mistress,
then of so tender an age that her work dragged
on the floor from her lap as she sat at her task.
Why Quacca had given the title of his father's
" young mistis " to Jackson Dawley's wife he
could hardly have told; but it was doubtless in
unconscious recognition of those traits which
gained for her some part of that consideration
which her humble neighbors commonly yielded
only to the quality. Indeed, Quacca loved to
seize any occasion for prostrating himself, and
genuflected with all the zest of the genuine African strain. His quaint contortions and grimaces
and the sounding gibberish of his cognomen
perpetually suggested his savage progenitors of
the Gold Coast. But he had developed a vivid
type of Christianity; and his lips distilled a
fluent piety as profusely as his drenched clothing
now shed water.

" Yes, mistis, Dimmis she needs ter get 'ligion.
I tells her, ' Dimmis, you 's a po' ole mustee
woman, but you kin seek for grace jus' the
same 's the quality; and once in grace allers
in grace, Dimmis. Thenk o' that now! ' But
she 's a dreffle sassy ole brack woman; she
ain't no 'spect 't all for 'fessors. I enters

inter my cluset, mistis, jus' 'cordin' ter what
the Good Book says, an' shets the do', same 's
the tex' tells on, to wrastle in pra'r befo' the
Lord, and she comes a bangin' agin the do',
an' a-screechin', 'Come 'long outer that kitchen
cluset, you no-'count ole nigger you! I knows
ye! You 'm gwine arter them pots o' 'sarves!'
Dimmis she hankers arter the flesh-pots allers,"
Quacca explained with figurative loftiness, adding in more matter-of-fact tones, "and them
was. real ginger, what Miss Mary brung down
herse'f from the big house when the ole woman
was sick. But laws! Dimmis ain't never suited.
She 's one 'o the discontented kine. I tells her,
'Ole woman, quiet down! Ye can't have squash
an' squealer together, — no, no, ye can't.'" (A
series of softly obsequious chuckles). "'Git
'long,' says she; 'don' talk no sich fool talk ter
me!' She ain't got no 'ligion, — not the fustest
notion on it. But 'pears like I could n't live ef
I had n't got 'ligion, bress the Lord! I ain't
got sich vittles ter home as you'm got here, mistis; but I 'se got 'ligion, hosanna!

> "' Oh, glory, glory, shout hosanna,
>   While my soul 's a-eatin' manna!'

'Ligion 's a gre-at thing, mistis; yes, yes, so
'tis; yes, yes." Quacca's burst of song was succeeded by the subdued chuckles with which he
emphasized his profession of faith, accompany-

ing himself, as it were, by sundry ecstatic bob-
bings of his apple-shaped head, while frequent
gurgles of satisfaction punctuated his soft, thick,
African utterance, his glistening canines express-
ing an animal glee, and his roving little eyes
betraying a furtive glitter, as though he scented
prey.

No sooner had his modest hints met with a
liberal response in the form of a basket filled
with such selections from the larder as the
returning Dawley might not miss than he discovered that it was no use waiting for the storm
to be over, for it was certainly the very one that
lightened up, thickened up, held up, cleared up,
and began again; and with a wealth of grinning
bows and thanks he took his punctilious leave.

The gloom of the autumnal storm shut Susan
in with her wretched thoughts; for the knitting
with which she tried to busy herself fell from
her helpless hands. Quacca's grotesque exhortations, instead of moving her somewhat torpid
sense of humor, had helped to stir into pulsing
life her dormant feelings of repentance. Perhaps he would not have been the most fitting
missionary to a saner spirit. How heartily either
Will Crowninshield or Jackson Dawley, each
after his own manner, would have derided the
idea of being moved to any less mundane emotion than a gale of laughter or a spasm of
disgust by the pious maunderings of an old

chicken-thieving hypocrite! But the gentle soul of woman is not so constituted that she can ever judge coldly of any appeal to her two ultimate sentiments, love and religion; and with her unquestioning reverence for all that stands for these ideals, he must be indeed a brutal suitor or a brazen Tartuffe who cannot entice her by the trumpery magic of his hollowest protestations, or convince her by the tinsel bravery of his cheapest lie.

"Poor old man!" mused Susan, with charitable thoughts of her late guest, and, as is the manner of people who have lived much alone, talking aloud to herself. "What a shame folks do scandalize him so! I believe he's a real good old man. How good he does talk! How he does love to talk religion! I wisht I could hev them good feelin's that he does!" sighed the poor, childish, ignorant woman, not blameless before the Judge of all hearts, but not of ignoble nature if scanned by the standard of human charity. "Oh! I don't believe I ever got religion," she cried, shaking convulsively in a passion of tearless sobbing. "I did go down them Jurden banks, ez the old elder said when we was all waitin' on the edge o' Cedar Pond; and Elder Stanton told me, 'Sister, onct you come up'ards o' them banks you'll see Jerusalem, an' you'll shout glory,' but I misdoubt there ain't no glory for me. I must be one o' them backsliders that is giv' over ter their own destruction," she whispered, shuddering at the possibility in which her religious teaching had instructed her of the desertion of the creature by an angry Creator. " Oh, I never meant to be so wicked in my mind, and hev sech feelin's, — ez ef I hated Jackson out an' out; an' then to feel — that way — ez I had n't no right ter — about — somebody else. Oh! I never half begun ter see how wrong 't was. Lord help me, why be I so set agin' Jackson? He 's rough-natered, but he ain't got sech a bad heart; he 's all wrapped up in the childun. Seems ez ef he 'd ruther hev them all ter himself. He don't want me 'round while he hes them; an' I can't feel 't he 's anythin' ter me now no more 'n I ever could. I don't hev no feelin's but wrong ones. Oh, I wish I was a stone! I·wish I was a corpse! Oh, my soul! Oh, my soul! Lord, save me!" she implored, wildly pacing the room as if to fly from some unseen foe, and, falling into the language long since grown familiar to her in prayer-meetings, she repeated, " Save me, O Lord, for the Enemy, the Enemy harries me!"   .

The rain dashed violently at the windows, and the gusts shook the infirm old homestead vindictively, as Susan mingled her weak cry of human distress with the Titanic voices of the storm; but it was none of these that arrested

her wild words. Slight as was the sound that
reached her ear, she started and trembled afresh
at the 'pattering step of her own child; then,
with a sudden rush of despairing tenderness,
snatched the little girl to her breast.

"Marmer, take Sukey; Sukey *tired*," fretted
the minute despot, whose pale little face and
lagging step effectively pleaded her cause; and
the small voice went on repeating her formula
in the same key of childish mournfulness, until
sobs gave place to comfortable yawns, and these
yielded to great sighs of content, as the throbbing little head, hot with play, and heavy with
sleep, rolled languidly upon the mother's arm.

The face that bent over the sleeper softened
to tears, and great drops moistened the parched
lids. A sigh that rose bearing the burden of a
penitent soul preceded the homely words of re-
solve in which the awakened woman pledged
herself to duty.

"Yes, mother will be good to you, mother's
poor little lamb. I won't be fretty with the
childun any more. I won't give way, ef I'm
ever so wore out; and I'll try to keep the house
fixed up; and I won't mope round so when
Jackson is ugly, — half the time he dono no
better; and I'll speak respec'ful ter Mother
Dawley, — she's a well-meanin' woman; and —
and — I won't think them wrong, shameful
things no more!"

Susan did not know that her tearful whisper was the truest prayer she had ever breathed. It did not begin with "Oh!" nor end with "Amen!" as when you made a prayer in conference meeting; which, indeed, was only accomplished by the shy Susan because she was too shy to neglect the elder's repeated intimations that we would all be glad now to hear from Sister Dawley.

With her little daughter's sleeping breath coming and going so close to her heart, Susan grew calm and soothed, and, in childish elasticity of mood, began to plan quite cheerfully for Jackson's supper. She would have hot flour-cake, with plenty of shortening, and she would get out the sugar quince; and there was nice cold ham, or perhaps she had better fry some liver. Jackson liked flour-cake, though he would grumble when he saw it, and would remind her that farmers' folks could n't live so high as them that had a trade. But she would take care to let him know, indirectly, that she and the children had dined contentedly on bread and milk. Not that he would deny them their choice of anything there was in the house; but he would be better satisfied so, knowing that the balance of household savings and losses had been properly adjusted. And she would try not to notice if he was a little rough in his way, and she must not be so silly and get nervous

when he beat the dog; it was all right, — Sport
needed training.

It all fell out much as she had expected; and
she was sitting wearily by the evening fire with
her work, — she and her husband sharing that
domestic solitude which Crowninshield had so
effusively anticipated for them.

Dawley, who had been working at a dismem-
bered gun, finally pushed it away with the air
of closing his labors for the night, and fell into
a study from which he emerged with a regret
that Mr. Crowninshield would n't be going gun-
ning over the Flats another fall. "I 'd ruther
ha' seen the last o' some o' the rest on 'em," he
announced. "He 's a free-handed sort, and he
minds his own business, and he ain't no fool
with a gun. I 'd ruther go gunnin' with him,
let alone the money, than with the hull lot. He
ain't no pride to him, nuther, Crowninshield
ain't," pursued this infallible observer, warming
to eulogy. "I tell 'um, he 's jest like common,
he is."

He paused in his praises, but no confirmation
of them came from his unfortunate wife. The
intelligence he gave was nothing to her; it
seemed already ages since that very morning,
but it was terrible to hear her husband speak
in this tone of unusual friendliness of the man
to whom she had given so many thoughts for
which she now suffered the pangs of repentance.

"We sha'n't see him this way again, I expect," continued Dawley, rather irritated by Susan's depressing silence; "he's gonter git marr'd, he says, this winter; and then they'll be travellin' quite a spell in the Old Country. Wal," with the short laugh, so like his mother's, which Susan so dreaded to hear, but was always helpless to avert, "I wisht he may light on some livelier company ter set up afore him than what a mummychog be's." Mr. Dawley puffed angrily at his pipe as though its contents had lost their soothing virtue.

Susan could not trust her voice, and the few words she tried to utter died hoarsely away. Her whole energy was concentrated upon the negative effort of restraining herself from a spasm of hysterical sobs. She need not have anticipated with such alarm her husband's curious observation. He had nearly dismissed the whole insignificant subject of his domestic life from his manly reflections. For a minute he had been annoyed at his wife's queer, nervous ways, and had said resentfully to himself that this was a nice way to behave to a man that always provided well, and never interfered 'round house. Well, as for Susan, she never was what you might call lively company, and something or other had come over her lately. Jinny Lewis, now. She was a live girl. She had her own way right along to home. How she made the

old folks stand 'round, though! he mused, ad-
miringly.   Folks found they'd got a cap'n when
. she was 'round, — dwelling with fresh interest
upon the high mettle, florid color, and redundant figure of that ornament to her sex, Miss
Angenette Lewis.   Dawley had none of his
wife's conscientious dread of forbidden speculations.   He thought of Jinny Lewis as freely as
he chose; often with a distinct regret that he
had not married her, and made an honest woman
of her; but as time went on, 'ie sensations
associated with her grew less potent, and the
ache of that old longing was well-nigh stilled.
Such profitless querying with the neglected past
soon gave way to plans for the next day's work
of hauling a jag of wood, and carting seaweed
for the Bull Meadow and sundry of the other
acres which, as it always irked him to remember,
had once been Susan's.

The silence of the house remained so long unbroken that the sounds of the night stole in
upon the two listeners.   The short sou'wester,
which had suggested a belated thunder-storm,
rather than an autumnal gale, had spent itself in
sudden plashes of rain, and gusty pantings that
fitfully tossed the creaking boughs of the old
buttonwood-tree, that labored in the wind like
a ship at sea.   The last of the fog was just dis-
appearing before the cold night-breeze, and it
was curling fleecily up from the woods and

waters that environed the Dawley homestead, rolling away in great masses before the moon-rise, and revealing the keen star-sparks that glinted with a wintry steeliness. The haunting cry of a loon came from the central solitudes of the lake, and Dawley, with a sportsman's instinctive action, rose to the tantalizing game.

"Change o' weather," he announced, as he opened the door and went outside to listen. "It's cleared away arter dark; it'll storm agin soon," he added, quoting one of those veracious weather signs that are not likely to lose their stormy-petrel reputation in our zone of intemperate climates.

"I hope not," Susan answered automatically, but with a great heart-throb that almost overcame the quiet of her manner. "All Thy waves and storms have gone over me," would have been the language of her spirit. She went to the door and still stood there looking dreamily out, after her husband had come in. How fair the beckoning distance seemed! How tenderly the moon-wake rested on the waters that gladly met the lustre that sought them out in the shelter of their evergreen shores. The trees passed to each other the whispered word of their nightly salutation. It meant refreshment, and peace, and joy, and aspiration. The aromatic freshness and softness of the vapors still lingering beside the cedar-framed lake, penetrated by the keen breath of

the living air that brought the wholesome influence of wintry purity, tempered the blood,
and soothed the sense. Susan's untaught per-
ceptions drank in the spirit of the scene, as surely
as clairvoyant eyes see the things that are hidden
from their ordinary vision.

" Wife," called Jackson Dawley, with a gruff-
ness that assuredly lent no very endearing intonation to the title, " did you furgit the doors hed
hinges onto 'em?   You 'm cooled off this room
a good one."

Susan turned with a guilty start, but her husband had already left the room, in which the lan-
guishing tallow dip just served to show the sordid
and grimy signs of a narrow, drudging existence,
and seemed, in that quick glance of hers, to cast
a sinister light upon the fortunes of its life-long
tenant. With a sudden impulse, as if the act
were a return to the freedom of her too short
girlhood, Susan looked again into the wonderful
world that lay beyond those closely crowding
hills. Somewhere there must be happiness in
life ; life must hold some of those things she had
dreamed of, but had never known,—such things
as easily belonged to him whom she did not
name in her thoughts, but who had unconsciously taught her what the world might be,
and what her world was. Somewhere, in the
distance, there was happiness for him and his.
But here might be peace. Here, below these

gentle, soothing waters. How grateful the sleep to be sought there when the weight of the day's burden grew too heavy to be any longer borne! She stood now between the living and the dead, —between the children who lay upon the hill and those who would soon follow them, from the beds where they lay sleeping. Oh, if she could but go now to join those, knowing that these must follow after her!

It was not an acknowledged thought; it was but an undercurrent of longing, stealing through the obscurer depths of the consciousness, while Susan still stood irresolute at the door, as if in the attitude of leaving the threshold to fare away, fast, and faster, out into the freedom and solitude of the great, wide, beckoning spaces of the whispering night. Her hand trembled anxiously on the latch as a childish voice of crying came to her ear, but she kept her place, as if by a spell. The sound was half-hushed, now, by indulgent tones, full of the pity and the anxiousness of fatherhood, and touched by the one influence that always tamed that rude nature. The woman's face suddenly softened from its drawn look of pain, as, with a quick, decisive action, Jackson Dawley's wife closed the door and fastened herself in.

"I had a little dahg, an' his name was Boof;
I sint him oot for a pinch o' snoof;
An' I think me story is long enoof."

"TELL some more, Pat!"
"Oh, Pat, do say it over real slow!"
"Tell it onct more, oh, do!"

"What's a-doin' here?" sternly queried the mother of the clamorously delighted audience as she briskly entered Farmer Hambly's kitchen. "Childun, guess you furgot yer comp'ny manners. I sh'd think sech gret gals ez you be mought ben ashamed ter raised day so. Run right away, now. Why, Pat Gallaghan, that you? 'T is Pat, ain't it?" pursued Mrs. Carr, putting the superfluous inquiry with a certain air of rustic condescension toward foreigners.

"Yis, mim," replied the young Irishman, rising with a crude attempt at deference, and seeking a moral support by fumbling with his hat.

"Why, dear suz, man! I sca'cely knowed ye!" affably remarked Mrs. Carr, whose visits at her brother's house were not of frequent recurrence. "Time I see ye afore 't wa'n't long sence ye

come over, an' ye don't look so dretful green ez
ye did" (with a broad smile of reminiscence).
"Don't wear them clo'es now 't yer brung over
from the old country, do ye?" she demanded,
frankly scanning Patrick's recent outfit, in which
the ruling tastes of his adopted country had been
duly consulted. The wearer received her allusion with beaming pride, while the lady, without
pausing for reply, went on, "Yer waitin' t' see
Danil? He's gawn up t' the Snuff Mill."

"Yis, mim, I har-rd, since I was in it, he was
afther goin' up there; but I tought he wud be
in prisintly, an' it was Misther Slocum bid me
give a missage till him."

"You ben up t' the Corners, an' going back
now ter Dutch Island, I s'pose? You'm far-
min' for Slocum right along now, ain't ye, sence
he come off the Island, an' went ter live with *her*
folks. Well, that's a pretty good lay fer yer,
Pat. I sh'd think yer'd feel real set up."

"An' ye've a right to say that same, mim,"
soberly agreed Patrick, with modest assurance.

"An' how's your wife, Patrick?" continued
Mrs. Carr, quite uninformed of any recently im-
pending domestic crisis, but merely on condescension bent, "say, how's Priscilly?"

"Thankin' ye, mim," returned Patrick the
straightforward, with a deference that was height-
ened by a certain air of proud solemnity, "me
wife was delivered of a young son at twinty min-

utes afther wan· o' the clock last Choosday mar-
nin' — glory be to God ! " and he crossed himself
fervently, all unaware, in his peasant simplicity,
that he had outraged the American proprieties,
and offended the matronly delicacy of his indignant hearer.   That lady did not stay to offer
congratulations, or to make further inquiries,
but left the room with an abruptness that can
only be described as flouncing out of it ; and
hurriedly returning to her place in the feminine
conclave of the sitting-room, gave loud expression to her disgust at the plain-speaking of " them
dretful coarse Irish."

Her comment failed, however, to make an
impression commensurate to that imparted by
her news. " *Tch, tch, tch,*" sounded from her
sister-in-law's sympathetically clicking tongue,
burdened with a rush of feelings that pressed
too strongly and suddenly to find their way
through the channels of articulate speech ; and
each woman of the neighborly circle added
some exclamatory fragment of utterance to
the medley response that greeted Mrs. Carr's
announcement.

There was danger that Patrick's error would
be overlooked, if not condoned, in the zest with
which they fell to on receiving this fresh morsel
of intelligence. The flutter and cackling, the
shrill confusion, and the pleasing dismay rife
among the party, suggested the reception by a

staid flock of hens of an ear of corn flung suddenly among them. No less interest could be
aroused by such an opportune event in a rustic
community, where the only really engrossing
romance-reading is that of the book of human
life, which, when daily conned, is a continued
story that has many a dull and tedious page,
many lapses and omissions, and many grievous
repetitions.

"Well, well, of all I ever *did*," breathlessly
exclaimed Aunt Hambly; "risin' a week old, I
do declare! and I never heerd a lisp on it," she
added, in the aggrieved tone of one who had
been defrauded of a culminating sensation.
"Well, times is changed. I tell 'um things
goes so queer now, in these new-fashioned
times, 't I don't know no more about my neighbors than —— than the child unborn," she concluded, rhetorically suiting her style to her
subject.

"What Priscilly was a-thinkin' on," bitterly
proclaimed Mrs. Carr, "to go an' be married
by a priest to a Paddy, and she Elder Hall's
own gran'da'ater, tries my possibles ter find
out."

"Well, you see," uttered Mrs. Hambly, in
deprecating excuse, taking up with increased
interest the familiar narrative, freshly illustrated
by the last piece of news, and going again, with
renewed satisfaction, over the beaten ground

of neighborhood gossip, "she was all alone,
kinder. She hed n't no own folks, an' her step-
mother said ev'rythin' she could lay her tongue
to about her, so 't Priscilly got all discouraged,
an' notioned that folks was ag'inst her. The'
wa'n't no real fault ter find with her, but she
wa'n't gifted t' airn her salt. She took arter
her mother's folks; they was all so — did n't
know their heads from their elbers, any on 'em;
but they was all clever folks, an' Priscilly was
real pleasant spoken. All the neighbors said
't was a livin' disgrace when she marr'd ez she
did; but I hed cha'ity fer her. Pat 's good-
lookin', fer Irish, an' stiddy, or stiddier 'n most
on 'em, an' gits toler'ble wages; I expect it
makes a good home fer that gal. She could n't
turn her hand to an earthful thing that would
make her any livin'. Time an' time agin s's I
ter my husband, s's I, 'Father, what 's goin' ter
become o' Priscilly? She ain't no more sense
'n that kitten;' and he 'd shuffle out on it, man-
fashin, an' when I hild him to, 'Well,' s's he,
'she mus' git marr'd.' An' lo an' behold she
did, — sech ez 't was. An' I 've heerd say she
makes out pretty well, consid'rin'. The' was ole
Mis' Bowsuns went over an' stayed with her,
— Priscilly alwas humored them old Charlestown squaws, — an' she told me she never see
sech a house fer wings an' holders, an' the
hearth swep' up neat 's a pin."

"She 'll want somethin' 'sides turkey wings t' live on," tartly commented Mrs. Carr, who was still smarting under a sense of personal indignity. "Must be gret sight o' vittles, Cynthy, in a Paddy house, t' be sure! Soup o' geese-heads, an' pin-feather thickenin', I rayther think! Them 's the kind of outlandish dishes the Gallaghans 'll learn her. The mice stands round with tears in their eyes in her cluset, I guess!"

"No, I — I guess not, Maria Jane," meekly ventured her sister-in-law, slowly running a knitting-needle through her hair, "I dono but what Priscilly 's comf'table, 's fur ez that goes."

"I hope ter my soul she 'll hev a good gettin' up," sighed the last speaker's daughter, a pale and delicate young woman, with restless eyes, and a nervous, anxious expression, who, as she spoke, had just laid her sleeping baby in the settee on rockers which served as a combination of cradle and chair for mother and child.

"Who 's takin' keer on the woman?" weightily demanded Nurse Crombins, whose professional engagement in the house was just closing, but whose imposing presence intensified the interest of the conversation, and finely sustained the dignity of the occasion.

"Well, *his* mother 's over there, I sh'd guess," hazarded Mrs. Hambly, with a manner that implied no attempt to extend the charity devoted to Priscilla so far as to include the Irish mother-

in-law. Nurse Crombins sewed on, in a grimly
neutral silence, but of Mrs. Carr it might be
said that she gave tongue with the energy of a
whole pack in full cry.

"*His* mother! Old Nora Gallaghan! Horns
an' hufs! I'd ez lieves hev our old Speckle ter
nuss me!"

"I was on'y wonderin'," hinted the nurse,
at whose measured accents the conclave was
hushed in respectful attention, "I was jest cal-
culatin' what kerrickter o' rags they'm put on
that child!"

An echoing murmur of mildly sarcastic intent
ran around the deferential group.

"Poor cretur!" solemnly pursued the nurse,
whose words came slowly, hindered by a port-
liness that lent itself to gravity and dignity of
demeanor rather than to the proverbial jollity of
the stout, "to think of her lyin' there, tied hand
an' foot, an' with nobody thet's hed experience
ter dress that child so's ter make human shape
on it, an' ter work over its head ter shape it ez a
head hes got ter be shaped, ter look decent."
This was the special fad of Nurse Crombins.
"'Course it's a nice job, I don't deny it's a nice
job," continued the artist in plastic humanity,
kindling with her theme, "an' them thet's goin'
ter spile it should n't lay a finger t' it; but this I
will say, thet there never was one o' my babies
but what I fixed up a real nice round head, —

round ez a harnsum apple, arter I'd worked on
it a spell.   You take their heads," she said, addressing the company in a raised voice, and with
an animated manner that was fearfully suggestive
of a Feejee cook detailing her choicest recipe,
" you take an' feel o' their heads, an' they 'll give
middlin' easy, like putty, ye know, and you c'n
fix 'em up any shape that suits best; but I like
'em good an' round.   The' was folks that I
nussed with onct down ter the Dugway.   I won't
name no names," — magnanimously declared the
narrator, who, indeed, knew there was no need
of further particularity with so well-informed an
audience, — " but she was the notionalist woman
't ever I nussed — dretful awd — an' she told her
mother she would n't hev me workin' so on that
child's head.   Well, s's I, 'course, ef the woman
is notional, notions must rule, s's I, but of all
possessed ! " pursued the priestess of the cult of
the physique, breaking into a high-pitched laugh,
eloquent of injury, " ter go t' the Dugway ter hear
on new idees an' fashins ain't what I sh'd proph-
esied.   'Cordin' ter my mind, you mought 's
well live out o' the world, an' done with it, ez
live up there in them woods," she concluded,
with another wrathful laugh, echoing of a rankling resentment.

"Well, you might 's well be in Gret Swamp
ez on Dutch Island," remarked Mrs. Carr, with
the exasperating calmness of an absentee in

whom long residence in an adjoining township
had cooled the fervor of native jealousies and
partisanships.

"Pat don't like bein' so fur from a priest, he
says, poor misbrung-up cretur," commented
worthy Mrs. Hambly, with a sigh of benevolent
melancholy. "How solemnizin' 't is ter see them
thet hes immortle souls grovellin' like the beasts
thet perish!" she continued in a thoughtful
strain.

"Yes," agreed Mrs. Carr, "Priscilly Hall was
courtin' jedgment an' no less, when she unekilly
yoked herself to an onbeliever."

"Let's hope 't won't light on her now," spoke
Mrs. Hambly, with matronly sympathy.

"We don't know what a day may bring forth,
Mis' Hambly," admonished the nurse, with that
air of lugubrious prophecy which was as much
a part of her due professional bearing as gravity
is the badge of an undertaker. "Ther' is years
when the women most all goes that way. Five
year ago — I reck'lect it ez ef 't was yist'd'y — ez
it mought be fall o' the year, like this, I was nus-
sin' ter old Reedy Bly Joe's, an' the woman was
smart 's I ever see one, to all appayrence, when
the fevier come on like *thet*, an' —"

"'T would n't be no merrycle," broke in the
severe and godly Mrs. Carr, leaving the nurse
aghast at the audacity of her interruption, "ef
jedgment should overtake them thet will live

with publicans and Romers. To think a gal o' her bringin' up should furgit where she sprung 'from! I believe it's our dooty ter come out from among them, and be ye separate, ez Elder Hines said in his exhortin' last Sabbath, now when popyism an' skepyism is a-walkin' about hand in hand, seekin' whom they may devour."

"Well, there's Danil, come seekin' what he kin devour fer supper, I expect," interpolated Mrs. Hambly, with surprising levity, "an' I ben so betwottled a-sottin' here talkin', 't I ain't sot table," and she bustled away.

The evening was well-nigh over, according to the neighborhood customs, when, as the household had again met in the keeping-room, Mrs. Carr's "watch-eye," as her sharp vision was known in the family, espied a light and a figure pausing with it, outside the door-yard.

"Do see, Danil," exclaimed Mrs. Hambly, whose glance had followed her sister's, "who that is comin' here at half arter eight o'clock!"

The excellent couple went out upon their old-fashioned porch to meet their visitor, who with equal promptness accosted them, while she was yet struggling with the picket gate which conspired with the rude gusts of the October night to hinder her progress.

"Come over afoot an' alone!" she shouted, with energetic pants, as she hurried toward them; "but I ain't come in the dark, anyway," she triumphed, as she displayed the barn lantern, and like Mr. Pope's shepherds rejoicing in the full moon, "blessed the useful light."

"Kine of a revolvin' light, ain't it, neighbor!" humorously inquired Farmer Hambly. "Sh'd think 't was the lantern to Pine Judy Pint yer hed ref'rence to."

"Now, father!" admonished Mrs. Hambly, in reproachful distress; and, "Hey?" vaguely gasped the guest, that honest matron being quite unaware of her picturesque appearance as the wind momentarily eclipsed her luminary in the flappings of her substantial petticoats.

"There, now, don't you mind him one bit, Mis' Baton," coaxed her hostess, tendering a superfluous encouragement; for, "I don't!" laconically responded the dame, further remarking "and I never knowed them that did!" — dismissing the unprofitable subject to inquire, with a breathless eagerness that evidently feared to have been anticipated in its proposed recital, "Heerd an'thin' from Priscilly Hall, that was, ter-day?"

"Why, yes," began Mrs. Hambly, intending to luxuriate in narrative; but Mrs. Baton hushed her with an imperative signal.

"Pat Gallaghan little knowed what news was a travellin' to-wards him," she announced. "He'd ben three days up 't the Corners. Slocum sent fer him to come up, and Slocum's folks kep' him there doin' odd jobs till this art-noon. I

see ole Mis' Bowsuns when she jest come off the
Island, 'long in the forenoon, an' s's she, 'By
Jo-by!' — you know how them old Charlestown
squaws will swear — '*I* call her a very sick woman;' an' towards night, when I see the hearse
goin' by, an' I run out t' ask D'rius who was
dead, fer I thought mebbe he was gettin' things
ready, 'The' ain't nobody dead jest now,' s's he;
'I'm on'y gittin' of it home from the carr'age
shop; but from all I hear, I shall have to bury
Pat Gallaghan's wife pretty soon,' s's he, and he
driv along. Thinks I, I'll let Mis' Hambly's
folks know te onct, fer I thought we'd oughter
go right over there, an' it might be so as Mis'
Crombins could make out ter go." She ap-
pealed deferentially to that potentate. " Say,
Mr. Hambly," she adjured, with recovered assurance, " don't ye think we better go? Can't
ye boat us over there?"

Farmer Hambly at once fell into the mental
attitude with which he met any proposition.
By his meditative air he would seem to have
dived deep into the crystal well of Truth, the
better to consult her as to his measured reply.
Finally rising to the surface, he conveyed the
judgment of the goddess in the leisurely announcement, —

" Wal, I would n't wonder much but what I
could."

Satisfied with the unobtrusive gallantry of this

response, the zealous Mrs. Baton turned to Nurse Crombins.

"Kin you make out without me ter-night, Lucindy," solemnly inquired that authority, referring the matter to the young mother.

"Oh, Aunty Crombins, I should *think !* " remonstrated Lucindy, with a nervously reproachful sob. "What *do* ye take me fer? " She ran out of the room and presently returned with a hastily made-up bundle, which she put in the nurse's lap.

"Give my love to Priscilly, an' tell her I sent thet little dress to the baby."

" Why, you 'm robbed yerself, Lucindy, hain't ye? " protested her almoner.

" Oh, no, I want the baby ter have it an' wear it. It's a real pretty one. Tell her I made every stitch of *mine* myself," she began with a glow of girlish animation that chilled again under the returning consciousness of calamity.

" Mother," calmly observed Mr. Hambly, who had apparently again taken counsel of the invisible nymph, and was prepared to repeat the oracle, " seems ter me you 'm a gettin' that bunnit on kinder hine side afore, ain't ye? " He surveyed his spouse with an abstracted air, as of one who diligently essays a judicial decision.

" Oh, land o' saints, so I be ! " she cried, ridding herself with a jerk of the cumbrous head-gear. " I 'm addled so I dono' what I 'm about."

"Bet' stay right where ye be, mother," advised her husband. "Yer git sick jest ez easy ez fallin' downstairs, an' they 'm got all the hospital they want over there."

"Mis' Hambly! I am fa'rly amazed at ye!" announced one who spoke with more than marital authority. "Who 's ter see ter *my* baby, ef you go off ter stay all night, fuzzino?"

"Well, well, I 'll give 't up," yielded the kindly soul, "but I did feel a drawin' to-wards that poor, dyin' child," and she broke down in undisguised tears.

"Cryin', be you, mother, becos I 'm goin' off with these here women folks?" queried Mr. Hambly, with a lightness benevolently intended to relieve the oppressive quality of the scene. "Why, don't take 't so hard 's all that. I sh'll be 'round agin, ef so be 't they don't run away with me." But this graceful homage fell unheeded at the matronly feet of the oblivious Mrs. Baton, and the preoccupied Nurse Crombins.

The ladies followed him to the shore, and the boat received the substantial forms of its master, his neighbor, and the nurse, stoutly riding the water even after that fat aunt of Brentford had clambered in.

"She ain't no tub," muttered Mr. Hambly, as he took up the oars and affectionately addressed himself to the only feminine object within ken of a figure to appropriate the encomium.

"They say," observed Mrs. Baton, after a brief space of silence, during which the enshrouding and engulfing glooms above and below seemed to have stretched out some invisible hand that steadily dragged them to a nameless goal, "that Priscilly hed railly sprighted up, an' took holt ter work ez ef she'd got some embition, 't last. And they tell how she was jest ez pleased an' proud's ef she'd marr'd one o' the town council theirselves; and ez fer Pat, he sets his eyes by the baby."

"Mfh!" retorted the nurse, with the scorn of a superior mind, "Priscilly ain't deeper'n the well, an' them shiftless Irish thinks all the world of a young son, ez they says, no matter 'f they ain't got the fust rag ter put on its back."

The words of the wise woman could not be gainsaid, and Mrs. Baton at once abandoned her feeble line of defence.

The influences of the night and the mystery of the waters were again unbroken for a little space by the doubtful harmony of human speech when —

"S'pose you knowed Pat's had that child sprinkled?" resumed Mrs. Baton, with signs of controversial disgust.

"Don't say! And Priscilly was knowin' to it?"

"What! Ain't yer heerd SHE was sprinkled quite a while back?"

"That so?" struck in Mr. Hambly, resting on his oars in a mild shock of surprise, and indulging in the worldly recreation of a prolonged whistle. "Wonder what old Elder Hall'd say ter that?"

"I sh'd think he'd *rise!*" wrathfully ejaculated the bearer of the intelligence.

"A pretty thing ter whistle at, Mr. Hambly!" rebuked the nurse. "An' you holdin' office under the church this minute!"

"Where was her *religion?*" demanded the other exponent of virtue.

"Wal," thoughtfully observed their escort, making the long slow sweeps that were favorable to meditation, "I see somethin' in print onct that kinder jingles with the subjeck, ez you may say." Mr. Hambly further prefaced his valued quotation by a diligent clearing of his throat. "'Twas in a sort o' play-actin' book was the saw, an' it run like this, 'What but love is a woman's religion?' I've tho't on them words consid'ble many times sence," pursued the speaker, who had delivered the phrase with a curious care, "ez I've lived along, an' I won't say but what the' 's somethin' in 'em."

"More shame *fer* you, then, Danil Hambly," retorted Mrs. Baton. "The church oughter deal with ye, an' make a public example on ye fer winkin' at sech onrighteousness. Ef folks could n't rise above Priscilly Hall's notions yer *might* talk!"

"Sho, sister Baton," said her plain-speaking neighbor, with a peculiar twitch of the mirthful muscles, and recklessly charging on a highly dangerous *cheval de bataille*, "yer ain't so hard-hearted by half ez yer purtend. Yer ain't no Baptis' born yerself, ye know. I c'n remember the time when yer was raised a Methodis' afore ever yer see the Deacon," broadly hinted this indiscreet theorist concerning the occult religious influences.

"That's neither here nor there," tartly began the lady, with a snap of the eyes which the faint glimmer of her lantern failed to transmit with all the force that might have been desired.

"Wal, here we be ter the Island, anyway," announced her antagonist, with a craven haste that betrayed an anxiety to capitulate on any terms. "I'll be over ter the lighthouse an' nef ye want me.".

The women climbed the crumbling slopes, struggling against the gusts that blew the dust-clouds of the Island in their faces, and crossed the turfy meadow that bordered on the peat-bog.

"Pat said how her name 'in religion' was Julye," observed Mrs. Baton, continuing the interrupted discussion.

"Oh, yes," assented her listener; "I knowed she was named Jul-ye Priscilly arter both on her gran'mothers and a silver tea-spoon apiece.

I 've heerd say the' 's ben the time when the' was a silver teapot in the Hall family."

"Gallaghan's folks calls her Julye, an' nothin' else," said Mrs. Baton, snapping the thread of reminiscence which her friend was just unwinding. "The Priscilly part on it never come handy to 'em; but they said Julye was a real Catholic name."

"Ain't it takin' up yer cross, Mis' Baton," sighed the other, "ter think how they'll bury that poor gal arter their fashion, with no fun'l sermon, nor nothin' ter show respec' ter the dead?"

"Yes, it's awful," lamented her companion. "Priscilly was simple, but she was ez good a gal ez ever walked the airth; an' now ter think that she can't hev Christian burial!"

Their sympathetic exchange of opinions was interrupted as they neared the little low-roofed farmhouse by the clamor of sentinel geese; and their knock was promptly answered by Honora Gallaghan, which sounding appellation was borne by a diminutive old woman, weazen and wiry as only old Irish women can be.

"Whereabouts be the woman, Nora?" asked the nurse, assuming her professional manner, and naming the sufferer by the official title which was always used in designating one of her patients.

Nora expressed a thankful sense of the kindness of their visit, and led them through the kitchen to the keeping-room, which according to rustic custom had been appropriated as the sick-room.

"Burnin' tug, be you, Nora?" queried the observant Mrs. Baton, as she noticed the smouldering peat-sods in the kitchen fire-place. "Well, I never!"

The art displayed upon the pictured walls of the keeping-room spoke a various language, and presented a curious mingling of the distinctive marks of race and creed. An engraved likeness of General Washington faced a violently colored lithograph of Pius IX. A looking-glass surmounted with the American eagle emphasized the national idea, and the usual funereal scene of tomb, weeping-willow, and mourner might be supposed to stand for that indefinite thing sometimes vaguely known as "the Protestant religion." At least the northern side of the room committed itself to nothing more distinctive than this. But the southern wall was much more pronounced in its indications; for it bore a shelf on which stood a plaster image of the Madonna, and near it hung a rosary. More neutral decorations were supplied by the cuts from the New York illustrated papers and the gorgeous fashion-plates that had been tacked up here and there; while the odd contrasts and analogies obtaining among the miscellaneously inherited belongings of Patrick and Priscilla might be still further noted

16

in the taste of the feverishly tinted lithographs, of which one represented Byron writing out a poem (in a neat, clerkly hand), and invoking the Muse, who looked over his shoulder in the person of some darkly jealous Marianna or Margharita; or the Yankee clock, in the lower half of which art had painfully transfixed a man, whose conspicuous and conventionally treated heart lucidly revealed the pendulum at every swing; or the devoutly mystical study of the Sacred Heart of Mary, very faithfully and anatomically rendered, with a lavish use of pigments. The room was made comfortable by sheep-skins laid down for rugs, some of them colored with domestic bark-and-herb dyes. Braided rag mats lay on the floor, and testified to the industry of the maker. There were also clean, rustling, corn-husk mats, such as were originally the handiwork of the Charlestown squaws; and one of them was lying just as it had fallen half-finished from the busily weaving fingers of the young housewife.

Nurse Crombins stood looking down at the patient, whose widely open eyes were vacant of recognition. "She ain't got her senses," muttered the nurse. Yet the two women uttered their comments with bated breath.

"Oh, nuss, ain't she changed beyond anythin'? I sh'd never dreamp' 't was her."

"She'm changed ez fast ez ever I see 'em

changed. You'd say she *couldn't* be less'n
fifty year old."

"She looks older'n my mother did the day
she died. Hark ter that, now!—of all the sufferin' sounds!"

The sick woman's features trembled piteously,
and an inarticulate moaning, in which was no
note of returning consciousness, finally shaped
itself into the low cry of "Oh, my soul! oh,
me! oh, my soul!"

"Do you b'lieve the 's somethin' or 'nother 't
grieves her poor dyin' soul?" begged Mrs. Baton, in an awe-struck whisper, and gazing dimly
through the sudden tears that had surprised her
well-seasoned self-control.

The nurse shook her head, with the decision
of long experience.

"Mostly things gits fixed in folkses heads
when they git so fur gone ez this," she explained; "an' they'll say 'em over an' over,
till friends goes distracted ter hear 'em. An'
Priscilly, she was a gret han' ter say 'My soul!'
Don't yer know how she'd look up jest ez
quick, 'f ye told her an'thin' p'tic'lar, lookin' so
laughy, an' her eyes a-shinin', an' so pleasant-
spoken, an' 'Oh, my soul!' alwas on to the tip
o' her tongue!"

As the image recalled by the nurse's words
rose to their minds, the two looked again by
a common impulse toward the bed, and the

helpless, death-stricken figure lying there; then
turned away, and asked after the child.

"It's the foine choild he is." affirmed Nora,
with pride, "and cries as sthrong as hear-rt
could desire; but at all evints he slapes ristliss
the night, an' his brathin' is quare."

"Queer! I sh'd think 't was!" pronounced
the nurse, on examination. "Ain't you no
sense 't all, woman! This child's comin' down
with lung fever. An' no wonder! Here's
where you'm kep' him right along, I s'pose,
right inter the draft o' this here old door."

"Ah, now! An' I niver moinded it! I
niver tought it cud hur-rt him!" and Nora laid
the finger of perplexity against her withered
cheek.

"Well, you see, Nora," Mrs. Crombins instructed her, "this ain't one o' your sort o' babies, altogether. He ain't gonto be tough ez a
pitch knot, fer he's part Yankee, and Priscilly
never was rugged."

"Oh, whativer will I do at ahl?" helplessly
lamented the guilty grandmother.

"Ef thet air child was one o' *my* babies," proclaimed the nurse, suddenly stiffening out of
neighborly kindness into a dignified, professional neutrality, and regarding the Gallaghan
infant with an abstracted air, as being one of
those unfortunate innocents consigned by fate
to the uncovenanted mercies beyond her dis-

pensation, " Ef 't was *mine*, I say, I 'd break up
that strictur' with mullen.   I 'd wet some mullen
leaves in milk an' water, an' bind 'em on the
chist, an' put drafts 't his feet.   That 's what *I*
sh'd do."

" But," vaguely implored Nora, " where is it
I 'd be afther foindin' this mullen the night,
mim ? "

" 'Course ef you hain't got it gethered, you
can't git it now, Nora," admonished the Yankee
neighbor, with a strong touch of contempt.
" But," generously resigning the claims of professional dignity, " well, see, you got some rye
meal ? "

" Rye male, is it?   An' Julia allays did be
käapin' that same in it."

" Well, you jest fetch me some meal, an' some
mustard an' vinegar, an' I 'll see what I c'n fix
up ter help the baby.   We 'm come ter stay with
with yer ter night, ye know.   There 'll be things
ter do here, an' yer 'll want somebody — ter
watch, yer know — yes," she said, with a glance
of experience toward the bedside, to which she
presently returned.

" How long 's she ben like this, Nora? " she
asked of the old woman, whose quaint features
were touched with the signs of that nobler language which grief writes even on the least spiritual type of countenance.

" Shure, she had a right to be will, intoirely,

ixcipt she caught cowld, jist. An' it's mesilf cud n't till how it happened her, for the pläace do be jist beautiful for hate, barrin' the cracks in the flure. But it was the day before yisther-day she comminced to bur-rn wid the faver fit to brek your hear-rt."

"What could ye think on ter do fer her, Nora?" queried the nurse with pitying curiosity.

"Shure, I sprinkled her wid the wather from the blissid will that the Riv'rind Mither bid me take, when I säarved the Sisthers of Sint Clare," was the innocent reply.

"H'm!" ejaculated the other, refraining, with remarkable self-control, from further comment. "An'thin' else come inter yer head ter do, Nora?" she demanded with chilling sarcasm.

"I gev' her the tay be times, when she cud sup it, an' I sint post haste for the docthor," answered the unsuspicious narrator. "The ould Docthor Shute it was kem till her before, from Wickford, but whin the käaper's bye wint afther him, they towld him, at the South Firry, the docthor had gahn in the vissel for Newport; but owld Timmy Rooney, that lives jist forninst, rin afther the mail wagon, an' sint wur-rd to the Wakefield docthor, — I niver can moind his name jist, bit at ahl evints he be that one they does be afther cahlin' Docthor John Hinry, — an' the coach jist cript an' cript along, siz thim that was in it, an' the docthor does be gahn aff, whin they reached the pläace. An, whin it's tin, elivin miles ye do be livin' away from the docthor, ye 'll brek yer hear-rt wid the lookin' an' the waitin'. An' I did be ixpictin' Patrick widout fail; I niver dhramed they had rason to kape him, an' he niver stipped fut widin the dure while she was sinsible, an' the docthor kem afther he did. An' whin he kem till her bedside, he jist luked har-rd at her, an' filt her pouls, an' tahked wid me aboot her, an' at last he siz, an' tur-rned away, 'It's no use, she's goin' through.' 'Ye lie, docthor,' siz Patrick (but it's me belafe he niver sinsed what wur-rds he was späakin'), 'me wife will be well again, plaze God.' 'No, me lad,' siz the docthor, späakin' till him qui-ite like, 'she's goin' through the eternal gates.' Thin, 'Nora,' siz he, taäkin' me to the wan side, 'Nora, for God's sake get me aff o' this island. Have yees niver a sail-boat here?' siz he, for 't was in a row-boat he was fitched over; 'for I want to stip me fut ahn shure an' get bäack to me sick päaple,' siz he; 'an' that's all I 'll ahsk of yees,' siz he," concluded Nora, who, with curious effect, persisted in gilding the doctor's Saxon speech with the sunny riches of her own redundant brogue. "So the käaper's bye wint off wid him to shure, an' I wint bäack to Patrick."

"Where *is* Patrick, now?" asked Mrs. Baton, in wonder at his absence.

"Ah, mim," sighed the old woman, "'t is yer-silf knows the min does not be like us; they niver sit an' sup sorra; but they wud be afther sthrivin' wid dith itself. 'T was long e'er he gev over ahl hopes; an' thin he ran wild to hear her cryin' out ahn her sowl. 'Mither,' siz he, 'I must go off. to shure an' fitch the praste till her;' for the praste was ixpicted at the Firry the night to marry Timmy Rooney's gur-rl to wan o' thim little Frinch byes that wur-rks in the facthory to a plääce they cahls Shady Lea. 'Ah,' siz I, 'niver sthir to go; shure the kääper's bye will go there beyant for yees.' 'No,' siz he, sthernly, 'me wife is no hiritic anny moore,' siz he; 'an' there's no hiritic of thim ahl shall stip a stip to do her a säarvice,' siz he; savin' yer prisince, mim, for repatin' that säame. Har-rk to the poor gur-rl! how she does be cryin' out!"

Priscilla's faint moanings had risen again to a sharper note. The nurse, exercising that last duty of her calling in dealing with the sentient body, lightly moistened her lips with a cloth dipped in water; but the sufferer shrank away from the careful touch, and her voice, already hoarse with the death-change, sounded that dirge with which she was entering eternity. "Oh, my soul, my soul!"

"Don't, Julia, don't be cahlin' out so, dar-lint!" implored the old woman, hanging over her in tremulous distress. "Shure yer sowl is

safe; shure ye mind how the praste baptized
ye, an' aised yer sowl of morr-tal sin. Don't,
for the love o' God, don't cahl ahn yer sowl
anny moore. Cahl ahn the Blissid Mither and
her Son; cahl ahn thim to resave yer sowl
in marcy! Ah! she 'll niver spake wur-rd
moore!" and' Honora's wailing. broke into a
shrill cry as, at sight of the sudden wave of
change that ran over the whitening, sharpening
features, she dropped heavily into her chair,
and rocked herself to and fro, with the hard-
wrung, dry-eyed sobbing of the aged.

"There, there, Nora," spoke Mrs. Baton, laying a kindly hand on the old woman's convulsed
figure, "don't you take on; it 's most over now.
Poor gal! she 's most through with her troubles;"
she soothed, as the first faint sound of the death-
rattle was rather divined than heard. The nurse
threw back still further the loosened coverings
of the dying woman's laboring chest. "She 's
breathin' from higher an' higher up," she said,
and made a slight sign to her companion.

Nora sprang to her feet with the action of
youth, and sped to a cupboard.

"What you want, Nora?" questioned Mrs.
Baton, following her. "Ken I help you any?"

"Ah, will do I know," rejoined Nora, with a
kind of solemn defiance, turning upon her, and
showing the candle she had just taken in her
hand, "will do I know that the likes of yees niver

belaves anny thin' o' this, but this is our belafe, an' what we belave, that same we sthrive to do." She closed the lighted candle in Priscilla's hand and held it there, first lighting candles at the head of the bed ; and thus awaiting the last moment, began to repeat the litany for the dying.

"Here they come," whispered the nurse to her companion, as the door opened, and Father Mulchahey, closely followed by Patrick, entered. Patrick fell on his knees beside the bed, and the agonized gaspings of grief rose mingled with the last ebbing sighs of mortality. The priest began the rites of his office, and the two neighbor women by one consent stole away, and left the still breathing clay of their countrywoman to the ministrations of the alien race and the foreign creed. They had not very long to wait before the shrill sound of the Irish death-wail gave them to know that the innocent soul of Priscilla had gone to seek a better country, even a heavenly.

IN the great sunny garret of an old gambrel-
roofed homestead, a child of not more than
eight years, but quaint enough to be in keeping
with the colonial atmosphere of her surroundings, sat frowning with self-importance over the
study of an heirloom diary, which, though written
in the neat and elegant hand of the seventeenth
century, presented frequent difficulties, both of
style and calligraphy, to the ambitious infant
who had just conned these lines, inspired by the
mortuary muse : —

> "Simon, my son ! — son of my nuptial knot !
> Ah ! Simon 's gone !   Simon my son is not !"

"Where had Simon gone, and what was ne
not? " demanded the literal-minded reader.
"Oh dear !   I don't think I like this poetry as
well as Sir Walter Scott's.   You can always tell
what *he* means."

Deserting the Puritanic effusion, and donning
a sunbonnet that had seen much fatigue-duty,
she made her meditative way out into the June-
brightened meadows that stretched almost from
the door.   A gaunt English mastiff, whose de-
monstratively good-natured air detracted from

the savage dignity of the mould in which Nature
has cast his race, came leaping toward her with
awkward delight. The master, whose avant-
courier he was, received from the child the for-
mal greeting due to a guest.

"How do you do, Mr. Felix? Will you be
pleased to walk in?"

"No, L. C.; I have come to take you out for
a walk."

Mr. Felix being averse to the conversational
burden that was assumed by those who habitually addressed the child by her double name of
Lucretia·Catherine, given her for a great-aunt
who insisted upon having it used in full, had
seen fit to denominate her L. C., which pseudo-
nym softened itself into Elsie when he was particularly complaisant.

"And now what have you been reading to-
day?" he asked, with the idle air of one who
had dedicated the lingering hours of the June
afternoon,

"Wherein no man shall work, but play,"

to such amusement as might be derived from
the society of a quaintly old-fashioned child.

"Writing, Mr. Felix," returned L. C., laconically. "I can read writing pretty well now,"
she added with pride. "I read in the old diary
some poetry about Simon. 'Simon, my son.
He is gone. He is not.' What does it mean,

Mr. Felix?" queried the student, with a corrugated brow.

"You must never ask the poets what they mean. That is very bad literary manners."

"But where had he gone?" persisted L. C., who was contentedly skipping along the driftway, or darting after crane's bill and blue-eyed grass. The breeze from the bay came freshly inland, brightening the faces and quickening the steps of the companions.

"There be strange lapses and omissions in your attainments, most erudite lady. Simon had gone to heaven," instructed Mr. Felix, mindful to assume a virtue if he had it not; "and if you are good, you'll go, too, some day."

"I don't want to go to heaven," responded L. C., unconcernedly, and intent upon her nodding nosegay.

"Those are pagan words for little girls," said her friend, severely.

"Well, it is just like church, you know."

"And why are you not happy in church?" inquired Mr. Felix, developing his Socratic method.

"Because I can't read there," returned L. C., calmly. "And it is dreadful when such funny things happen. The old gentleman in front of us when he ought to say *throughly*, — in the Psalms, you know, — always reads out 'Wash me, though roughly,' and I want to laugh so it

is quite painful," complained the child, shaking
her head, querulously.

"Indeed, an exquisite pleasantry." Mr. Felix was guilty of a yawn.

"Was n't it ?"— eagerly. "I laughed so,"
related L. C., "that I had to put my head down
as if I was saying my prayers."

"Fetch me my tablets!" spoke Mr. Felix, to
an imaginary servitor. "My tablets! Meet it
is I set it down that feminine dissimulation
doth flourish and abound at the tender age of
eight years."

"Now you are talking like the wits," observed L. C., thoughtfully. "Yes," she nodded
emphatically, "a little like Mr. Pope, I think,
or perhaps a little, a ve-ry little, like Mr.
Addison."

"I will endeavor to hold my reprehensible
brilliancy more in check. But tell me something you like about church."

"Oh, I like it when 'they sing, ' Ory, ory, ory
fresh us,' because that is the last hymn, you
know. Mr. Felix," queried L. C., with sudden
earnestness, "does the Episcopal Church go as
far back as Washington? Old Mrs. Piper says·
so; and she and Mrs. Barker, that they call
the Baptist Barker, had high words about it
the other day, Sally says. I knew he was the
father of his country," pursued L. C., "and I
thought perhaps he might be one of the fathers

of the church, too.   I 've heard about them. Do you think so?"

"You ask me too much, as your townsfolk say. I could n't settle so nice a question. I would rather ask you what you have been doing to-day besides reading."

"Oh, I 've been sitting in our graveyard," answered L. C., with animation.

"Young Mortality. What takes you there so often?"

"Because I like to make friends with the gravestones," replied L. C., on reflection.

"Do you never play with any children, my child?"

"Why, there are n't any for me to play with, Mr. Felix, except seven miles away. Sometimes when we go to church I run away to play with Mary Scarlet, but they all say, 'Do you know what day it is?' or else Maleen Castle — out in the kitchen you know — says, 'What a cantico them children do make!'"

"Who is your friend, did you say?"

"Mary Char-lotte," repeated L. C., with visible effort.

"Oh! How odd it seems that you should still have babyish struggles with your articulation. So you don't care much for play? Where is your doll, now? I 'm afraid you have no feminine traits."

"Why, you said I was too feminine, just now,

when you talked like the 'Spectator,'" remonstrated L. C.

"Your memory is as inconveniently good as
Sintram's. (Ah, heard your name, and pricked
up your ears, did n't you, old fellow?) But certainly, every good little girl should be learning
something useful every day."

"Well, I am sure I sewed my stint." (She pronounced it *stent*.) "But Sally said such stitches
were a sight to behold, and a living disgrace to
my name. I *did* hurry, for I wanted to go out
and pick kingcups. Sally says if I don't learn
to sew better my name will ring when I grow up.
She says it will be heard of clear from one end of
the town to the other."

"From Little Rest Hill to Little Comfort
Cove," idly muttered Mr. Felix, hazarding a
local allusion, and blundering in it, as strangers usually do in such rash attempts.

"And I made a pat of butter," gravely announced L. C.

"Really! Come, that is doing very well,"
commended her monitor, benevolently.

"Yes, I ran away up to old Dora Driscoll's,
and she let me do it. Sally is so cross; she won't
let anybody into the milk room. 'Go and scald
your hands first,' Dora said."

"Not a bad idea that, L. C., for I have seen
them when they were not above suspicion, and
quite grubby at times."

"They were pretty grubby, as you say, Mr. Felix," calmly assented the young lady, "that day we dug the 'saxifrax.' But you know it was early in the morning, and the dew was on, and so, when we got through,

> "'I washed my hands in water that never rained nor ran;
> I dried them on a towel that was never wove nor span.'"

"That reminds me that I brought you some deleterious candy from the store, at your own native cross-roads."

"Oh, how nice, Mr. Felix! Now we can sit down here by Alph, the sacred river (you know that's what I've named Injun Run), and eat it together."

"Very well, L. C., am I not your devoted slave? Certainly, we will partake, and we will be poisoned together; just like two young Parisian lovers, with a sociable pot of charcoal between them."

"How funny you are, Mr. Felix," she chuckled, animated by the equally stimulating qualities of the candy and the wit. "I like you to be funny.

"Don't you think, Mr. Felix," she queried after a pause, "that your noble hound looks you in the face as though he would have you say, like Sir Philip Sidney, you know, 'Thy necessity is yet greater than mine'?"

"L. C., your inveterate pedantry embitters a man's most careless moments. Here, Sintram!

This is commended to your more robust digestion. Tell me, Elsie," continued her instructor, "have you none but a bookworm-ideal?"

"Oh, yes; I wish I were like Miss Phœbe. I think she is just perfect."

"Because —?"

"Because she wears a belt," answered L. C., promptly.

> "At Kilve there was no weathercock.
> And that 's·the reason why,"

quoted Mr. Felix.

"That 's in Wordsworth," nodded L. C., with a satisfied air; "I 've read it."

"You dreadful child, you have read everything and learned nothing."

"I like Wordsworth," pronounced L. C., decisively. "And Byron," she subjoined. "And Anon., the old English poet in the 'Farmers' Almanac.' And I like Shakspeare, too. But you know, Mr. Felix, that Mr. Rowe thought he was only a kind of a wild, irregular genius."

"Keep strictly to the classic Miss Phœbe, just now, L. C., and read me the charms of her cestus."

"Of her chain, you mean? (I suppose that 's a word for chain.) She has lots of little charms on her watch-chain, and she wears her watch in a beautiful silk belt, all colors, and her hair comes way down each side of her forehead,

and just clears her eyes, and covers her ears
all up. And she never pushes it back behind
her ears, if she's ever so busy. She says 'Yes?'
and 'Yes, indeed,' when you tell her anything—
and 'He's nicely,' when you ask how her father
is — just as sweet as — as cream candy. And
she keeps it so nice and smooth a fly would slip
up on it, Sally says. Sally says there's nothing
proud nor haughty about her, and you never
would know, to see her so free and pleasant in
her ways, that her father keeps the store, and
she wears a real Dunstable. When she is going
away from our house Sally always comes in to
'take leaf' of her, she says, to show how much she
thinks of her, and how 'she'll uphold her anywhere, for a girl of gold.' She tells Miss Phœbe
she's going to speak a good word for her some
day, and Miss Phœbe always laughs, but they
won't either of them tell me what it means, except that it's lahro for meddlers."

"Well, never mind that grievance, L. C. Let
us go back to the interrupted story of your an-
cestors, as you gathered it from your old book
in the garret."

"Oh, yes. I told you Simon's mother died.
She was very beautiful, and had the small-pox,
and all the children died, and had it, too; and
Simon's father says: —

     "'In splendid beauty she did much excel,
      But the small-pox did it and her expel.'

" Did you know, Mr. Felix," breathlessly continued L. C., " that Cap'n Seecoke had come
home from New York with the small-pox? "

"I am just now made aware of it by your
artless narrative."

" Is n't it dreadful? "

" Yes, it is sad to think that he lacks an accomplished poet, like your ancestor, to cele-
brate his malady in soothing verse. Now I
understand the full pathos of the saying, 'They
had no poet, and are dead.'"

" Old Dora has been in it often, for she says
it 'did be very *breef* [prevalent] in ould Ireland.'"

" Your conversation has taken on an agree-
ably foreign flavor of late. It used to be largely
seasoned with the provincial Sally. What was
the last thing she said to you? "

" Why, she only called to me out of the
cheese-room window just now when I ran by
that my head looked ' like a hooraw's nest.' She
thinks I ought to keep it as smooth as Miss
Phœbe's, and I can't! But she did n't drag me
in, because she was keeping Seven Day."

" What is that? "

" Why, Sally was brought up with Sevendy
folks. Have n't you heard her say so? And
Saturdays she sits in the cheese-room and sings
her hymns. When I would n't come in she just
shook her head at me, and went on singing the
baptizing hymn, —

> "'Go down to the water if you 'm dry,
> And there you 'll get your full supply.'

She always says I shall come home drownded.
She said something about *you* the other day,
Mr. Felix. I don't know whether I 'd better tell
it."

"By the way, L. C.," asked Mr. Felix with a
carelessness so profoundly studied that he failed
to hear the last remark, "about how old do you
take me to be?"

Nothing surprised by the change of subject,
the child regarded him intensely with a business-like air, frankly making a telescope of her
hands the better to scrutinize his features, and
cheerfully announced at last, —

"I guess you 're about as old as grandfather."

"L. C.!" harshly exclaimed Mr. Felix, flushing
angrily, and half-rising, only to resume his place,
as if reminded of his dignity, "if you ever joked,
I should think you were joking now. I believe
I had forgotten," he added, forcing a painful
smile, "that you had not come to your common-
sense yet." He got up and walked moodily
about.

"Why, Mr. Felix," loudly reasoned his un-
flattering companion, "to be sure, you 're not as
gray as grandfather, but you 've got those funny
little markings all round your eyes just the same
as he has, only," she confessed with another prolonged gaze, "not quite so many of 'em. And

grandfather is n't as old as I used to think; for
he can't remember the Trojan war; he told me
so when I asked him once. But that was a great
while ago," she explained, " when I was twice a
little girl. I did n't know any better then."

"Know henceforth, L. C.," proclaimed her
friend, again summoning that constrained smile,
"that I am still young and blooming. I had
a birthday yesterday, and I was only thirty-
nine." Mr. Felix, after due search, drew forth
a folded paper, and complacently smoothed it
on his knee.

" Oh, did somebody write you poetry on your
birthday?" demanded his young friend, with
enthusiasm.

"Well, yes," admitted Mr. Felix, with becoming modesty, and proceeded to read: —

A BIRTHDAY SALUTATION — ADDRESSED TO MYSELF.

The melancholy day has come, the saddest of the year:
With spirits low, in accents grim, my title all too clear
I read upon Time's balance-sheet, where sundry dates
    combine
To write me down seized and possessed of years just
    thirty-nine.

Embarrassed by my riches, I fain would shift this
    treasure
On shoulders yet ungifted in such abounding measure.
Ah, could I but dispense it, I 'd ask no dole of labor,
But all my fortune freely I 'd settle on my neighbor.

My deed from Time I cancel, and fund my years in com-
   mon!
Right nobly I resign them, and spurn the wiles of Mammon.
I' hail this just conclusion with socialistic glee,
And I shout in dates and seasons for wildest anarchy.

Oh, much it irks me to recall that ofttimes I forbore
To sound the scornful interdict, "Pshaw! forty odd or
   more!"
High words of dauntless youthfulness!—but still they
   may be mine:
Be swift, my tongue, to launch them while yet I'm thirty-
   nine!

"What do you think of it?" inquired author
of critic.

"Well, I don't know," hesitated the child.
"Was it written to be funny?" she ventured
dubiously.

"No, L. C.; it is steeped in depths of Dantean gloom."

"Oh, I *thought* you read it like that," she returned, brightening up at this confirmation of
her judgment. "Thirty-nine," she nodded,
with an air of recognition; "yes, I know it in
the tables."

"Ah, you'll know it better by-and-by, when
you've been longer in the great school that has
no vacations."

"But I don't go to any school at all," said L.
C. with dignity.

"True. You have not begun to learn. You
do not know where you are living, my child."

"Why, Mr. Felix, I heard grandfather say only last evening we lived in School District Number Thirteen. Uncle says that in Providence, where he has stayed so long, they call it the South County down here. But he says they don't know much up there in Providence."

"Ah, I thought you did not know. This is Arcady."

"Why, no; it is n't." ("The dwellers in Arcady never know their fortune," mused Mr. Felix.) "But I know how to get there," insisted the other; and as her listener turned idly toward her she was encouraged to inform him at puerile length that the stage had Arcadia painted on it, and must run there, though it appeared that Sally insisted that "wheresumever that might be, it never run no nigher to it than Branzinewuks."

"Mr. Felix," she inquired, without sign or warning, "is thirty-nine too old to be in love?" Her companion turned a self-revealing look upon her as she coolly proceeded, "Because Sally says you must be crossed in love; for nothing else would keep you moping 'round here so long. She says it's 'mor'n 'markable he should make such a harmit of hisself.' But excuse me if you don't want to tell!"

"Why, I believe I was just going to confess to you, Elsie," smiled her friend, if rather ruefully, yet with a genuine air of relief. "Yes, I am much obliged to Sally, and I put full faith in

your discretion, for you are a loyal little soul.
Not a word, you know, to anybody about it.   It
shall be our secret, just between ourselves,"
he admonished, and was answered by glowing
looks of a speechless devotion that almost overpowered the gravity with which he had begun
his narrative.

"Yes, I will submit my fate to you," repeated
the speaker, in a mood between jest and earnest.
"You shall be my Queen of Love and Beauty
(let me brush off that envious rose bug); and I
will inquire of you, for you are already more
deeply read in romance than I ever had time to
be.   You shall tell me why my wooing does not
prosper.   This is the case, briefly stated: Is
thirty-nine too old to be loved by three and
twenty?"

"I guess not," was the prompt opinion of the
court.   "You see, Mr. Felix, twenty-three is
pretty old, too, and I don't think she could
mind; especially as you can't live so very long
now," L. C. added, soothingly.

"Exactly.   So you approve?"

"I don't *quite* know, after all," she objected,
with a knitted forehead.   "There was a story
last week in the ' Pendulum ' about like that."

"Did it turn out well?"

"Oh, beautifully!" cried L. C., eagerly.   "At
least it *ended* good.   He was very old, most as
old as you, I guess, but he was *so* good; and he

died at the foot of the first column, and then she married the one she knew before — the young one — at the foot of the next column, and they were very happy for almost a quarter of a column."

" I am afraid I could never be as high-minded as that, L. C.   In fact, if that were the only way to be good, I should never go in for being good at all."

" But you must, you know, if you really love her," L. C. gravely declared. " You ought to be going into a decline, — yes, hurrying into one, — or, if you cared for her very truly, you would somehow get yourself thrown from your horse, after you had made your will very handsomely. And if you wanted to do it all in just the best way, you would never once let her know that you loved her at all, — you would be so careful to save her feelings."

" My little queen, this knowledge is too wonderful and excellent for me; I cannot attain unto it."

" But, perhaps she will like you best, in the end," consoled L. C. " Sometimes it turns out that way, too.   And you are so much like Fitz-James : —

> " 'On his bold forehead middle age
>   Had lightly pressed its signet sage,'—

Only," she soliloquized, " to be sure, Ellen

did n't fall in love with him; it was young Malcolm she loved."

"You are rather unfortunate in your instances. But still, my child," continued Mr. Felix, in the tone of soft playfulness that lightly veiled the truth of his intent, "all discouragements aside, would you advise me to write to her and tell her that I love her?"

"I would, yes, I would, dear Mr. Felix!" cried L. C., with unusual warmth of sympathy. "Do write her one of your nice funny letters, just as you wrote me when I had the scarlatina."

"My dear little girl," he replied gravely, "I can't take your kind and flattering advice, much as I wish I could, because — well, for one thing, because I 've done it already," he was fain to conclude.

"You mean you have written to her?" demanded L. C., with childish persistence.

He nodded moodily.

"And she does n't answer?" asked the child, reading his face.

"And she does n't answer." Mr. Felix twirled the willow switch he had idly stripped of its leaves, and cruelly beat down a dying swath of innocent buttercups.

"Well," said L. C., cheerfully, after a moment of cogitation, "perhaps she has n't got any ruled paper. I wanted to write a letter myself last week," she pursued, with an important air, and a glance aside, to see if her dignified labors were duly recognized, "and I could n't because there was n't any ruled paper, and black lines under-neath were no good.

"Or perhaps," she resumed, on finding that her friend's gloomy silence remained unbroken, "your letter has gone wrong. Did n't you mail it in the wrong time of the moon? Sally said last month 't was a 'Saturday's moon, and come it once in seven years, it comes too soon.' She said her granny told her so. Or don't you think perhaps her letter to you has gone wrong?"

"No, L. C.," said Mr. Felix, wearily rising, and slowly pacing by "the sacred river" of her naming, which babbled a merry undertone to their serious debate, as it ran bearing their trib-ute of leaf-pluckings and flower-strewings "down to a shoreless sea," "that only happens in your stories. Besides, I have heard from a friend, who mentioned that she was going abroad at once. That does not look as if she cared much for us, my poor Elsie." He smiled rather grievously.

"Oh, the letter is lost; I am sure the letter is lost!" wailed L. C., beating her palms together. "Why, it always is down a crack, or under a step, or something. It has dropped somewhere; they always do. Only yesterday I read a story about a letter that stayed a month in a corner, behind some cobwebs.

"At any rate," she prattled, finding her con-
clusions indifferently received, "if you mean to
be married before the twelvemonth's end, you
must swallow a chicken's heart whole.   That's
what Maggie Driscoll did.   She says it's a
charm; but she would n't give me one; she said
I must wait till they had chicken again. 'Whisht,
niver moind!' she said (what makes Maggie
talk so funny, Mr. Felix?), she'd do another
charm, she said; and she boiled an egg, and cut
it in two to take out the yolk, and filled up
the shells with salt; and I could n't eat mine;
but Maggie ate hers, 'for to dhrame of her shu-
tors,' she said.   But she was cross all the next
day because she only dreamed of big Mick in
the ould country, and she don't care a ha'p'orth
for him, and she says 'must she be spending her
wages to fetch that gossoon over here?'"

"That will do, L. C.; your conversation de-
teriorates; I shall take you home."

> "If you talk before you go,
>   Your tongue will be your overthrow,"

quoted L. C., from Sally, who, as it appeared,
often reminded her that her babyhood had been
marked by this stigma.

L. C. was in skipping spirits all the way home;
and her friend put aside his graver mood to take
elaborate leave of her at her door.

"Adieu, Lucretia Catherine; fair creature,

adieu." And he bent in burlesque devotion over the morsel of a hand.

"Good-by, Mr. Felix; and now remember I 'm sure the letter was lost," she declared in her shrill pipe, and with a commanding frown.

" 'Sh, Elsie," warned her departing guest, and laid a finger on his lip; but he did not look altogether disheartened as he turned away.

"Oh dear, I am sorry he has gone!" sighed L. C.; "and I wish," she murmured sadly, as she felt in her empty pocket, "that I had n't eaten up all the candy."

She was intensely surprised to learn the next day that her mature playmate had left the place early that morning.

Several weeks later she was flattered with a sense of importance by getting a letter duly addressed to Miss Lucretia Catherine, but reading somewhat less formally within: —

EXCELLENT L. C., — Thanks, praises, rewards, devotions, homages! Excuse my Gallicisms; but this is no time for dealing in the cold Saxon idiom. Faintly at best can I express, my adorable infant, what I owe to your inimitable insight — clairvoyance, I may call it — which led me to the treasure that lay *perdu* in the keeping of that gruff custodian, our mutual "Uncle Holder," who controls our epistolary fortunes at the cross-roads. Often had I besieged him before with inquiries after this particular letter; and it was against my (fancied) good sense, and in spite of my pride, that I went to him from you on that happy day when your persistent assurances that it was lost helped to restore my faith in its existence. Our Uncle was surprised, surly, reluctant, but fortunately there are means of soothing without compromising official dignity ; and after the needful amount of grumbling he made the exhaustive search that I relentlessly superintended.

Do you remember Captain Seecoke, and his small-pox, of which you told me ? By his perversity in falling ill of this malady just as my letter came to the office, I had nearly lost all the dearest hopes of my life ; for the dove-like little missive was swept away by the great, cumbrous, gallinaceous wings of the " Bird of Columbia," the political weekly that the Captain most affects ; and it was thus unconsciously deposited in his letter-box ; and there it remained from week to week awaiting his convalescence. The accumulating papers would not be delivered sooner, as no one could call for them ; and as long as no letter arrived for the Captain our learned Uncle judged it not worth while to send up his mail by the doctor, since the patient might be supposed to be suffering a temporary suspension of interest in the exchange of political hostilities.

After this, I shall acknowledge a sympathy with your ancestor, and, if I had his pen, I would, like him, present the claims of small-pox to be married to immortal verse.

If you expect my narrative to flow as frankly as one of your favorite stories, Elsie, and if you ardently desire to hear about my letter, I can only meet your wishes so far as to say that you must gather enough from what I tell you in relating that it was an inspiriting one — if read between the lines. This sort of invisible writing is such as you will probably understand better by-and-by ; but it seems that the writer of the letter, when she did not hear from me, concluded that I did not know how to read this fairy cipher. I am afraid I stood very low indeed in her estimation just then, Elsie ! At any rate, she tells me now that it was because she had not been understood that she was going away from us all. She had convinced herself that she ought not to have left anything for the interlinear interpretation, and had I been a day later, it would have been too late to find her on this side of the Atlantic. So near should I have come to losing all — but for you, and your pretty faith in the ever romantic.

Now, my dear little girl, mind this : When I shall come to see you next fall, with my bride (that now is to be), on our way to Newport, be ready to accept and return the love of a lady who holds you very dear ; and believe now and always in the devoted affection and gratitude of your faithful servant,

FELIX.

University Press: John Wilson and Son, Cambridge.

www.ingramcontent.com/pod-product-compliance
Lightning Source LLC
Chambersburg PA
CBHW031925060726
47496CB00007BA/1986